A MOTHER'S HEART

SWEET HEARTS OF SWEET CREEK #6

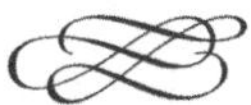

CAROLYNE AARSEN

CHAPTER 1

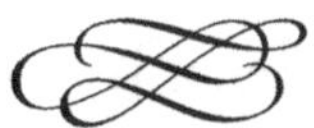

"Emma, I'm not fooling. It's time to go," Claire called out as she slipped her purse over her shoulder then grabbed her daughter's backpack from the kitchen counter.

But she heard nothing. No giggle from her daughter pretending she was lost. No whine from their dog, Mooch, wanting to go outside. Emma wasn't in the apartment.

Her heart jumped and she struggled to calm herself; the endless burden of being a single parent clawing at her.

Relax. She's probably outside.

In spite of her self talk Claire hurried down the narrow hallway, locking locking the deadbolt, giving the door an extra pull to make sure the wonky lock worked. Her feet tapped out a rushed rhythm down the worn concrete stairs.

As soon as she stepped outside, she heard Mooch barking and Emma calling out for the dog.

But Emma and Mooch weren't playing in the dirt-packed yard of the apartment building and, as she listened her distress turned to annoyance.

Emma and their dog were in the neighbor's yard. And there was a new tenant in the house who probably wouldn't appreciate unwelcome visitors in the form of a little girl and a dog.

Just as she was about to walk around the fence dividing the properties, Emma's called Mooch's name over and over. And then she started crying.

Claire's mother instinct kicked in. She ducked through the small gap in the decrepit wooden fence, her eyes skittering over the yard.

Emma stood by the swings, sobbing her little heart out. Claire dropped her purse and the back-pack and rushed to her daughter's side.

As she did, she noticed a man in the far corner of the yard, hanging on to Mooch's collar, re-straining their over-exuberant lab. He was tall and lean with brown hair. Easy on the eyes, but his face was creased with lines of irritation.

"Honey, what's wrong? Did you hurt yourself?" Claire dropped to her knees in the long, damp grass. She checked Emma's face and her neck, looking for bruises or bumps or worse, blood. She seemed okay.

Emma's sniffed, settling down as Claire pulled her close.

"That man is being mean to Mooch," she cried.

Claire glanced at "that man", who struggled to keep his hold on their dog.

"I was inside the house and I saw your dog digging in the flower bed," he explained, holding onto the collar, answering her unspoken question. He had a deep voice. Resonant. His t-shirt strained over broad shoulders and muscled arms. Claire fought down a flicker of appeal, forcing her mind back to the current situation. "I tried to stop him," he continued. "That's when I saw your little girl playing on the swing. She started crying, and the dog started barking."

His frown deepened as the tone of his voice grew defensive. Even though Claire would soon buy this property, if this guy was renting the place, it was technically his; her daughter was trespassing and so was their dog. His annoyance surprised her, however. Most renters didn't care much about the yards. Or flower beds. Especially not male renters. Especially not someone who would be moving out in a week and a half when Claire purchased the house.

"Mooch is so sad," Emma wailed. "That man has to stop choking him."

Still confused, Claire released Emma and her daughter ran over to Mooch, dropping to her knees and wrapping her arms around the dog's neck. Mooch whined and pulled, his head bobbing as he struggled to get loose from the man's grip.

She could see the man was about to let Mooch go.

"Wait," she called out, running toward them. Mooch was still a pup. A large and exuberant pup who would easily drag Emma across the yard.

Claire reached Mooch and Emma just as the man released his hold on the collar. Claire grabbed for the dog but was tripped up by Emma, who struggled to hang on to Mooch. The dog spun around to lick Claire, pulling her around and sending Emma flying. Claire tried to reach her but the dog knocked her over.

And as they tumbled down in a flurry of legs and arms, Claire fell against their new neighbor.

He caught her by the shoulder, spinning so she landed on top of him. She lay there a moment, stunned. Then, realizing she was lying on top of a stranger, Claire struggled to her feet.

Mooch must have thought they were playing and jumped on top of them and Claire went down again.

Finally the guy got to his knees, taking Claire up with him as she fought to regain her balance. For a moment they kneeled, facing each other.

Up close he was even better looking. Thick lashes framed deep brown eyes shadowed by a frown, his mouth unsmiling but appealing. Stubble shaded his strong jaw and his thick hair was awry. Claire felt a wayward desire to straighten it.

She shook it off, pulled herself free and got to her feet just as he caught Mooch again. Emma stood beside them, her head tilted to one side.

"So, lady, could you please get control of this critter?" he said to Claire, the irritation in his voice justified but still a tad annoying. Technically, it wasn't her fault.

"Sorry. I'm so sorry," she said, breathless now as she brushed her pants, looking with dismay at the streak of dirt down the front of them and her once-white shirt. She looked back up at him, her cheeks on fire.

"Is Mooch okay?" Emma asked.

Thanks for the concern for your poor mother, Claire thought.

"Mooch is in trouble," Claire said firmly. She turned back to their neighbor. "I'll take him now."

The man blew out a sigh then shoved his hand through his hair, messing it even more. "Just hang onto him. I don't want him to get away again. He's done enough damage." Claire took Mooch, and as their neighbor walked over to the corner of the yard, her heart sunk.

The flower bed was now a mound of dug-up dirt, some spread out over the lawn. Bricks from the edging had been torn out and the remains of hollyhocks, lilies and various other plants littered the rest of the bed. Mooch had done a real number on it.

Claire had helped Mrs. Blatchford, the previous owner of the house plant many of those perennials because some day the house, the yard and this flower bed would be Claire's. She and Mrs. Blatchford had drawn up an Agreement for Sale giving Claire first dibs at purchasing the property. Then Mrs. Blatchford, in her generosity, had also given Claire six months to pull a down payment together.

All summer Claire had watched from her apartment window which overlooked part of the yard, as the flowers bloomed, creating an ongoing display of color and beauty that Claire enjoyed from afar, knowing that soon she could look out of the kitchen window of the house and see it up close.

It had taken her the full six months to save most the money she needed for the down payment. The last few thousand would come when her cousin paid her for her deceased husband's irresponsible choice of a sport's car.

"I'm sorry about what Mooch did," Claire said to the man who still looked annoyed.

She didn't blame him. She was annoyed, too. One more thing for her to fix up once she bought the house.

He nodded, then frowned as he held her gaze. "You look familiar. Didn't your parents own the hardware store in town?"

"Still do," Claire said, puzzled as she struggled to remember him.

"Sorry. I used to live here," he said, pointing to the house. "I'm Nik. Nik Austen."

His name sounded familiar but as she tried to place him, something else he'd said registered.

"Used to live here? In this house?"

"For a few years."

Claire scoured her memory and a hazy picture

emerged of a tall, gangly boy with unkempt hair and a ripped shirt walking up the sidewalk of this house.

The house Claire, Tess and her parents used to live in. The house that held Claire's fondest memories. The house she hated leaving behind when their family moved to a larger, more modern home on an acreage just out of town.

After her family moved, Claire would bike down her old street from time to time, taking the long way home from school, just to make sure the new owners were taking care of the house she so yearned to return to.

The new house was all angles and glass and metal and, even worse, often echoed with the angry voices of parents arguing over a purchase, she realized later, they couldn't afford. This house, with its dormers and bay windows and porches front and back, had been more of a home to her than the new one.

"That's right. But you never went to school here, did you?"

"I was home-schooled by my foster parents," he said, his voice taking on a cold, hard tone.

His comment reminded her of the wild stories the boys at school made up about him because they seldom saw the kid living in Claire's old house. They said he was crazy. Maybe even a murderer. That's why he never came to school. Whenever anyone did see him, he looked untidy and angry.

Then, after a couple of years, the family sold the house to Mrs. Blatchford and moved away. Nik and his odd family faded from everyone's memory.

"And now you're back?" Claire asked.

"Yeah. For a while. I guess if I'll be your new neighbor I should introduce myself," Nik said, his mouth curving into a half-grin that belied the previous tone of his voice. His smile enhanced the shape of his mouth and created an appealing fan of wrinkles around his incredible brown eyes.

Claire shook off her reaction, realizing she hadn't returned his courtesy. So she took his hand, hers engulfed by his. "Sorry. I'm Claire. Claire Donnel — sorry — Kruger." Though she'd been on her own for five years, her married name still slipped out at times. She had switched back to her maiden name when Andy walked out on her and Emma.

"Good to meet you," he said. "So you and your husband live next door in the apartment?"

"My daughter and I do. My husband passed away a year ago."

"I'm so sorry," Nik said.

"Don't be. You didn't know." Claire waved off his apology, stifling a flare of shame at her evasive answers. It had been difficult returning to Sweet Creek as a single mother, abandoned by the man who felt he 'had' to marry her when they found out she was expecting Emma. Claire thought she was in love, so she had agreed. But as soon as Emma was born, Andy couldn't deal with it all and left. Now that her ex-husband was dead she felt she could pass herself off as a widow.

"So you're only here for a couple of weeks?" she asked, feeling the need to be at least a little neighborly even as Mooch tugged on his collar and Emma lingered, swinging her purse around.

In ten days, Claire would sign the final Purchase Agreement on the house and take it over. She was surprised that Devon Grey, Mrs. Blatchford's son, agreed to such a short-term rental.

"I'm here to connect with my mother and sister. See how it goes."

Another memory solidified.

"Nik Austen. You're Cory's brother. Joyce's son." Cory, her friend and part-time helper at the cafe Clair owned, had been over the moon excited when her fiancé, Matthew, had found Nik. All her life Cory had lived in the hope that the brother her mother gave up for adoption would come back into her life.

And now, here he was.

"Have you seen Cory yet?" she asked. "I know she was gone for the weekend."

"We're meeting tonight." He sounded evasive and Claire understood that finally seeing his biological mother would be difficult for both him and his mother.

"We should go, Mommy," Emma said.

"Of course." She had lingered long enough. "I hope you enjoy your stay in Sweet Creek and again, I'm sorry about what Mooch did to the flower beds."

Nik shrugged. "It's okay. I'll get Devon to knock some off the selling price for the damage."

Claire almost gave him a polite smile and turned to leave but what he'd said caught her attention.

"Knock some off the selling price? What do you mean?" Claire's breath slipped out of her and her thoughts were a jumble of questions.

"I'm buying the place. It's not a done deal yet, but we're working out some kinks. Apparently there's an Agreement for Sale in place right now but the conditions on it will run out in a week and Devon Grey doesn't think the buyer can meet them."

Claire's heart thudded. Her head spun. She was the buyer Devon didn't think could meet the conditions. She was the one who needed to meet them in a week.

"You might buy the house?" she asked, surprised at how even her tone was.

"Not buying the house. More like buying the property. It's a great location and a huge piece of real-estate. The house is junk though. I'll tear it down and build a fourplex if I can get the town to zone for that."

"Tear it down?" Again, she sounded like an idiot as she processed what he said. She had to leave but she couldn't let go of their conversation.

"Yeah. That's what I do. Either fix up a house and flip it or do an infill. Been doing it for years." He spoke to her like she was a rather slow child. "But this house isn't worth fixing, so I'll do an infill. Then I'll take the money and head out again."

Panic clawed its way up Claire's chest at his casual dismissal and assumption that his plans would go ahead.

She had to contact Devon Grey. Immediately.

"Mommy, I should go to school," Emma put

in, practicality taking priority over Claire's confusion.

Claire shook off the dread clenching her stomach, pulling herself back to the task at hand. "Can you get your backpack and Mommy's purse and bring them to the car?" she asked Emma, jerking her chin toward the bags lying on the grass by the swing set.

"I can," Emma called out as she skipped off.

Claire turned back to Nik trying to tamp down her fear, her heart pounding. "I gotta go. See you around." She spun around, sucking in one breath after another as she walked back to the fence.

She felt as if she had been hit in the stomach.

Devon had another buyer for the house. A buyer who wanted to tear it down. Why didn't he tell her?

Don't panic. Don't panic, she reminded herself as she slipped through the hole in the fence, her thoughts a painful jumble. A few phone calls would straighten this out.

"Mooch wasn't a very good dog, was he?" Emma asked when they were on the other side of the fence. "I hope he's good for Gramma when we bring him there."

Claire closed her eyes a moment to center her

spinning thoughts, turning to the next thing she had to deal with.

"He'll be fine." She didn't really care if Mooch behaved.

Her mother was the one who gave the dog to Emma for her birthday this spring against Claire's express wishes. However, Mooch couldn't stay in the apartment while Emma was in school and Claire was at work, so Mooch got to stay with Claire's mother during the day.

"Are you okay, Mommy?" Emma asked as Claire took her purse from her daughter, rummaging through it for her car keys. "You look mad."

"I'm fine," Claire said, her tone short as she struggled with her wavering emotions.

"Am I in trouble for going on Mrs. Blatchford's yard?" Emma's voice quavered.

Claire pushed her frustration aside and gave Emma a tight hug. "No, honey, you're not. It was a mistake, that's all."

"I'm sorry Mooch made a mess of the flowers."

"I am, too," Claire agreed, stroking Emma's fine hair away from her face and dropping a gentle kiss on her forehead. "But it's done and maybe we'll have to help Mr. Nik fix it up."

"He probably doesn't know about the lilies," Emma agreed as Claire opened the door of the car. Mooch jumped in and settled on the blanket on the seat and Emma climbed into her booster seat.

"He probably doesn't," Claire agreed, waiting to make sure Emma was buckled in before closing the door.

Before she got into the car, she shot a quick glance back at the house. To her consternation, she saw Nik standing on the back deck of the house, watching her.

Right at that moment, the memory of lying on top of him in his yard flashed back. She shook off her humiliation and walked around the car, got in and drove away.

Thankfully Tess had offered to come in that morning and do the baking to give Claire a welcome break but she was now behind her schedule. Instead of bringing Emma to her mother's she would have to bring her directly to school herself, then drop Mooch off.

She walked her daughter through the doors right as the bell rang for class. Claire had hoped to talk to the teacher to see how Emma was doing. Since she'd started Grade One, Emma had complained about a sore stomach and headaches.

Vague symptoms even their family doctor had a tough time diagnosing.

But she had no time today.

As she hurried back to her car she dug in her purse for her cell phone to explain to her mother the change in plans.

But her phone wasn't there.

She frowned and scrabbled in her purse more, then checked the car. She remembered putting the phone in her purse before she made Emma's lunch.

Then she realized where it was.

Lying in the yard where she dropped her purse when she ran to help her daughter.

The yard she had hoped would be hers one day.

The yard that Nik Austen, Cory's brother, might end up owning.

* * *

So, that wasn't the best first impression, Nik thought as he raked up the dirt that ridiculous dog had spread all over the grass.

He could only imagine what was going through the mother's mind. *Claire's* he corrected, allowing himself a moment of appreciation for the lovely woman.

Who had landed on top of him.

She smelled like almonds and honey and her hair was silky soft.

And stop there, he told himself, dismissing his wayward thoughts, raking harder. Though his plans had changed the past month, they still didn't include a woman. Especially not one with a child.

For now, he had to take care of this flower bed.

Normally, plants weren't high on his radar. For the past ten years he had never lived in a house long enough to concern himself with the landscaping. That was done after he'd either done the renos on the purchase or torn it down and in-filled. And then sold again.

But he'd been feeling melancholy the past couple of days. Two months ago, Rebecca Huizinga, the elderly woman whose home had been a haven to him after the dark chaos of living with the Baley foster family, had passed away.

And he missed her.

She always had such beautiful flower gardens and encouraged Nik to help her take care of them. Rebecca would have been impressed by this one. Though fall was approaching, and some of the plants were brown or dead, he recognized many of them. At least the ones that still stood — no thanks to that undisciplined dog.

Which made him think of the little girl.

When he saw her playing on the swing, his heart clenched. Emma was the same age his baby would have been.

The baby his ex-girlfriend had swept out of her womb and their life without a second thought. And without telling him.

He had never understood how Theresa didn't think he should have any say in the matter. In fact, he had found out after the fact. He would gladly have taken care of their baby, even if Theresa didn't want to. He knew what it was like to be abandoned.

His own mother had given him up for adoption when he was four years old.

The same mother who now lived here in Sweet Creek and who had, through a lawyer, reached out to Nik to connect with him.

Nik finished raking the dirt, glancing at his watch just as his cell phone rang.

He checked the screen. His buddy, Chance.

"So what bad news do you have for me now?" Nik asked, walking back to the porch to sit in the shade. Though fall was coming the sun still had a lot of strength.

"Hey, that's no way to talk to your oldest friend."

"Some friend. Ducking out a trip we've planned for months. We were supposed to be diving in Cozumel right now."

"I had asked for that time off. I was told it was a done deal. Not my fault my father-in-law said he made a scheduling mistake and told me I couldn't leave." Chance sighed.

"You need to work somewhere else," Nik said. "That's not the first time he's gouged you like that."

"I'd work with you if you weren't such a flake," Chance returned. "Or if you'd be willing to stick around in one place longer than six months."

Nik ignored the jab. While Nik had always found regular work as a carpenter/contractor every place he worked, he never found a place where he'd wanted to stay and put down roots. Nor did he have any desire to. Easier to be the one to leave than to be the one left behind.

"So, where are you now?" Chance asked.

"Sweet Creek."

"Where is Sweet Creek?"

As Nik tried to find the best way to answer,

his knee jittered. He stopped himself, angry at the nervous gesture he'd developed when he turned eight. When, for the second time in his short life, his world had fallen apart.

"Apparently, it's where my biological mother lives."

Nik had never any desire to look for his biological mother. He was four when she dropped him off at Social Services, gave him a hug and warned him to be a good boy. Waiting for him were Audry and Karl Jensen. A couple who hoped that adopting him would ease their unhappiness. However, taking in Nik only increased the tension between them and it burst out into the open when Nik was eight. They divorced, and Nik was tossed into the foster system.

It took three homes before, at the age of nine, he ended up at the Baleys' place. They moved to this town, Sweet Creek. Into the house behind him.

And thus began one of the darkest periods of Nik's life. Abuse, neglect, nights spent banished to the basement, being yelled at, hit — all this became his new normal. Until he got moved at age twelve to Rebecca Huizinga's house. He lived with her until he turned eighteen.

But he never forgot his birth mother. Never

forgot that day when his life became a dark, lonely place for so long.

He never forgave her, either.

"Sweet Creek is in the Kootenay mountains." Nik stood and walked away from the house, turning so he could see the mountains that rose above the valley where the town nestled. Mountains he used to stare at from his window when he was banished to his room. Mountains he'd dreamed of climbing up and over to get away from there.

And now he was back.

"So you found her?"

"Actually, she found me. Now, after all these years she wants to connect."

"And she lives in Sweet Creek?"

"Her and a sister whom I never knew I had."

Chance exhaled, his confusion easy to read even over the phone. "A sister. You have a sister."

"Shades of Luke Skywalker, right?"

"Is the force strong with her?"

"Haven't met her yet. Or my mother. Cory was out of town when I got here. I called my... called Joyce when I came here but she was rather flabbergasted. Told me she wasn't feeling well, and could I come another time. That was Saturday, shortly after I got here. She gave me Cory, my sister's number, then hung up. Cory's next on my people-to-call list." Her and the real estate agent who he was dealing with on this property.

"It might have been a good idea to let them know you were coming," Chance said. "She might not have been as much with the flabbergasted."

"I suppose. But still, Joyce was the one who reached out to me. I thought she was ready to see me."

"Seriously, dude, you need to do better prep work. You can't just jump into someone's life and expect them to switch gears that fast. It's been a lot of years, you know."

"I know. I guess I should have called," Nik conceded, rubbing his forehead with the palm of his hand, the pangs of a headache forming. "Didn't think that would make much difference."

"So are you sticking around there? Spending time with her?"

"Well, now that I'm not going on this long-planned trip with my best buddy, Chance, I've got all this free time—"

"Stop hassling me about that. I've apologized enough about it. I lost out on an amazing trip of a lifetime, too, you know." Chance was quiet a moment. "So, what you gonna do there? In Sweet Creek?"

"I have a project."

"Of course you do. Tell me about it."

"I talked to a real estate agent to see if there were any short-term rentals. I chatted with this Alan Andrews guy. He told me about this place. How it's for sale." Nik paused, surprised at the rush of anger and fear this house could still create. At first, he didn't want to have anything to do with it. Asked Alan to find him something else, but then he drove there and parked in front of the house, looking at — annoyed at — the hold the Baley family and that house still had on him.

When he saw the condition of the house and the size of the yard, he made potential plans.

"Don't tell me. You bought it."

"It was a steal. Sweet Creek is becoming a premier resort town. It's close to an awesome ski hill and some great fishing and swimming lakes. Lots of hiking and mountain biking trails. I gave the owner a low-ball offer, and he said he would take it. It's not a done deal, though. There's someone else who has an Agreement for Sale but the owner doesn't think they can meet the conditions. I'll know on Monday. Less than a week away."

"And there's no way you'd fix it up? Stay

there? You've got two good reasons to put down roots."

"Not a hope." His answer burst out of him, harsher than he'd meant it to be.

When Nik first entered the house, he was annoyed at how all the old fears and fury returned. The helplessness, the deep, choking anger.

Though it was furnished with leftovers from the previous owner, Nik had slept on the couch in the living room. There was no way he was going anywhere near the rooms upstairs. The room where he would spend hours locked inside after he was bad. The room where he suffered too many blows from a drunk foster father. Too many angry tirades from a foster mother who often said she regretted taking him in.

He found out later that the only reason they took him in was for the money.

Chance sighed his disappointment. "I guess I keep hoping that one of these days you'll find-"

"My forever home?" Nik returned with a sardonic tone.

Chance had been married once and though his wife passed away he often talked about finding someone someday. He encouraged Nik to do the same. Settle down. Make a home.

Nik's thoughts slipped to the little girl he saw

a few moments ago, and he felt another unwelcome stab of sorrow. And another reminder of why it was best to stay single. Pain, loss and disappointment were part of every relationship he'd ever had.

"Anyhow, I'm here now and if everything goes through I've got work for the next few months. Months I was supposed to be holidaying with my friend."

"You can still do it."

"By myself."

"Will you fix it and flip it?"

"Nope. I'll do a tear down. I can put two houses on this lot or a fourplex, it's that big."

The thought of taking the house down gave him a peculiar satisfaction. It could be symbolic. A breaking down of the old. A way of eradicating memories that still haunted him.

He could give this property a fresh start. Better memories.

"How long will it take?"

"Nine months if I can get the sub-trades lined up."

This way he could give his mother and his sister an opportunity to get to know each other. And he could be on his way, free from all the entanglements of his lonely, empty past.

"So what if you and your mother don't hit it off?" Chance asked.

The same sinister thought had occurred to Nik. "If not, it will give me a good chance to get to know my sister at least."

"Is she your full sister or half?"

"I don't know. Other than my mother, she's the closest thing I have to a relative. I'd like to get to know her better. And, this property was too good a chance to pass up."

"Too bad I can't help you out with the work."

He and Chance had done a few house flips and renovations together in their heyday. Before Chance got married to Donna and started working at his father-in-law's business.

"Like I said, you could quit your job." Nik leaned back against the step, looking out over the yard and the mess in the corner, still annoyed with that silly dog.

"I could."

"You should. Your boss was the one who ixnayed the dive drip."

"I know. I guess I like security."

A gentle dig at the lack of stability in Nik's life and future plans.

"Anyway, I've got enough going here to keep

me busy awhile," Nik said. "If this deal goes through."

"So how will you manage all this? A tear down and rebuild?"

"I'll move my trailer on the yard. You should see this place. The yard is so big I could start an RV park and still have space. Besides, if I'm on site, I can keep a better eye on the sub-trades."

"I can't believe you like living in that thing. Cramped and temporary—"

"And cheap." Nik got up and walked over to the now-destroyed flower bed. It hadn't been there when he'd lived in the house. And he wanted to make sure it stayed because it reminded him of his now-gone foster mother.

"Someday you need to settle down, mister. Find a place and make a home for yourself."

And share it with who?

"I should go," Nik said, his tone abrupt. "And if you need a job."

"Only if you're looking at settling down."

Nik knew enough to leave that alone. "Anyway, take care."

This was usually Chance's moment to tell Nik he was praying for him. Something Nik's foster mother always said, but this time around, Chance just said goodbye and ended the call.

Nik held his phone, frowning at it, wishing his friend would lay off the hints about settling down.

He dropped his phone in his pocket, grabbed the shovel and finished fixing up the dirt in the flower bed. When he was done he straightened, noticing the gap in the fence. That would be the next thing he would fix. Last thing he needed was the dog and that little girl sneaking into the yard again.

He was about to head to the house when he caught the glint of something in the grass by the play center. Curious, he walked over to check.

It was a phone. As he picked it up he saw the pictures on the case. They were of the little girl that had just been in the yard. He guessed the phone belonged to Claire. He held it a moment, wondering what to do. Then it quacked like a duck and a text message flashed on the screen.

Hey sis, are you playing hooky today or are you coming? Coffee Creek is crazy right now. Get your adorable self here quick. Cory is helping but I have to duck out.

His heart did a small jolt when he saw Cory's name.

The same name as his sister's. And he guessed,

in a town the size of Sweet Creek, there weren't an abundance of girls named Cory.

* * *

Nik angle-parked his truck on Main Street, taking the first empty spot. He wasn't sure where Coffee Creek was located but it was a nice day for a walk and he didn't think it would take long to find the cafe in the small town.

Grabbing the keys, he jumped out of the truck then paused, struggling with second thoughts. He thought of what Chance had said. He hadn't told Cory he was coming. But he pushed them aside. He had to deliver Claire's phone anyway.

Before he could change his mind, he strode down the sidewalk, past other town residents who didn't seem to be in any rush. Large concrete planters full of flowers that still bloomed bright pink, blue and yellow were interspersed along the street and more prominently on the corners at the intersection. The streetlights were older, Victorian style, which blended well with the inlaid, brick sidewalks and brick buildings lining the street. Multicolored flowers spilled out of large pots suspended from the streetlights.

Sweet Creek looked better than it had when he and the Baley family lived here.

Which meant he should have no trouble selling the houses he hoped to build.

He passed the hardware store, a couple of women's clothing shops, Allen Andrew's real estate office, a bookstore, a store that sold bikes, a bakery, a pharmacy and a variety of other stores, all busy. No boarded-up windows, and there were lots of people on the street coming in and out of the businesses. Some he recalled from his time in Sweet Creek, but other than the hardware store, the pharmacy and the Stop 'n Shop at the end of Main street, he didn't recognize the rest.

Just ahead of him a couple of metal chairs and tables huddled under a yellow and white-striped awning and as he came nearer, Nik saw the name, Coffee Creek, etched in silver on the double doors.

His sister was inside that building.

His palms were damp and his knee jittered once again. Angry with his reaction, he stepped forward and pushed open one of the doors. A jingle of bells announced his arrival.

First, he noticed the long counter running along the far end with glass cases full of sandwiches, wraps and pastries. On the wall above the counter was a large chalkboard with the prices and offerings written out in fancy lettering. A few flourishes decorated the corners. Clearly a woman's touch.

Wooden tables with mis-matched chairs filled the space. Other than an older couple at one table, drinking coffee, the place was cozy but empty.

However, it was the woman behind the counter who caught his full attention.

Claire handed a man a paper cup of coffee, smiling at something he said. Her brown hair was held back with a bandana which emphasized the arch of her eyebrows and the exotic tilt of her eyes.

And just as he was about to approach the counter to hand over her phone, she looked his way. As her eyes found and held his, he remembered the scent of her hair, the weight of her on him. And an unwanted jolt of attraction ran through him.

But her smile slipped and then became forced.

"So, we meet again," she said, her voice holding a faint edge. He guessed she was still angry with him over how he'd made her daughter cry. And how he'd treated that silly dog of hers.

He got to the point and handed her the cell

phone. "I found this in the yard. I figured you might want it back."

Her mouth shifted from a smile to a frown, as she reached for it. "I'm sorry. I realized I had lost it when I got here. Thanks for returning it."

She flashed him another tight smile, reaching up to tuck a stray strand of hair back behind her ear. "Can I give you a coffee? On the house? As a way of thanking you for bringing me my phone?"

Nik glanced up at the board, scanning the offerings then gave her an apologetic look. "Sure, I'll have a coffee, but I can pay."

Claire shook her head. "Not a chance. You brought me my phone."

"It wasn't a big deal."

"No arguments," Claire said.

"I'd listen to her," a voice cut in. "She's one ornery lady."

Nik turned to the woman who had joined them. She was tall, slim, and her wavy hair was held back in a loose ponytail.

His heart thudded as their eyes met.

The same dark eyes as his looked back at him, the same unevenly arched eyebrows. The same hint of a dimple in one cheek.

And the same stubborn cowlick on her forehead as the one he struggled with.

This had to be his sister.

She stared at him just as he must have been staring at her.

He saw her swallow, her hand coming up to her mouth.

"Hey, Cory," Nik said, breaking the awkward silence.

"Nik," was all she could say.

They stood there a moment, the counter a barrier between them.

"Cory, why don't you go have coffee with your brother," Claire said, her voice quiet. "It's quiet here now. I can manage."

Cory blinked, still staring at Nik. Then she broke her gaze and glanced over at Claire. "I… uh… I guess."

Nik felt a tremor of unease. He wasn't sure he was ready for this.

But isn't that why you are staying here? To see your sister and mother?

Cory glanced once more at Claire who looked at her with sympathy. As if she understood how awkward the moment was. Cory turned around and walked to the back of the coffee shop, disappearing behind a door.

"She's just going to change," Claire offered.

Their eyes met and once again Nik felt the

unwelcome attraction. Then, Claire blinked and looked past him to someone standing behind him.

"What can I get you, Mark?" she asked.

"Sheryl wants a steeped tea and I'll have a chai latte. They're both to go."

Nik realized he was impeding her customers, so he stepped aside. Mark, a tall, rangy looking man wearing a plaid shirt, blue jeans and cowboy boots, gave him a cordial grin then pulled his wallet out of his faded pants. He looked like a cowboy.

"You sure you don't want to stay?" Claire asked.

Mark shook his head as he handed Claire some cash, waving off the change she held out. "We're on our way to the pediatric specialist."

"I hope it goes well," Claire said, tucking the change back in her cash register. "I'll be praying for you and Sheryl and your baby boy."

"That means a lot." Mark took his drinks and as he turned, he met Nik's eyes. Mark gave him a brief smile then hurried out.

Claire's comment made him think of his foster mother. She was always praying, too. Always trying to get Nik to do the same. Oh, he went through the motions, but only to please her.

He wasn't big on all that faith stuff. Didn't help him in the past. He doubted it would help him now.

Then a movement beside him caught his attention - his sister was back.

His sister. The thought still jarred.

"Do you mind if we have coffee here?" she asked, her voice soft, her eyes now averted from him.

"Not at all."

"We can sit over here," she said, walking around a corner to a secluded table for four, hidden from the rest of the coffee shop. "Few people like this table because it's too private. Most everyone who comes here wants to chat and be a part of the ambience. I don't always work here but I'm helping Claire out for today. Her sister is gone. Wedding plans." She stopped, looking apologetic. "Sorry. Babbling. I'm kind of nervous," she said.

"I'm not going to lie, I'm feeling the same," Nik admitted, appreciating her honesty.

He wanted to say more but Claire was beside them holding a tray. "Your usual," she said, setting a foamy latte in front of Cory. "And coffee for you," she said to Nik. "Unless, of course, you prefer a latte? Sorry I never asked."

"Coffee is just fine," he said.

She set his cup and a plate of squares and cookies on the table.

"Thanks, Claire," Cory said, flashing a genuine smile this time.

"And it's on the house, so you two don't need to fight over who's paying."

Nik glanced up at Claire to thank her, catching her gaze. And once again, that distressing attraction returned. He blinked then looked away, dismissing the distraction. He wasn't allowing himself to get involved with another woman.

"So. Here you are." Cory cradled her mug with her hands, hunching her shoulders in a defensive gesture as she gave him a delicate smile. "All these years."

Nik wasn't sure what to say to that so he nodded, taking a sip of his coffee, his stomach tightening.

"So tell me, how did you find us?" she asked.

"Some lawyer named Matthew McKnight was calling my lawyer. Then this Mathew guy got a hold of me. That's how I found out where you lived."

Cory gave him an enigmatic smile. "That Matthew guy is my fiancé."

"You're engaged?"

"Yes." Her smiled turned shy as she looked down at her hand. That's when he noticed the diamond on her finger. So now he not only had a sister, he had a future brother-in-law.

If he wanted to lay claim to that.

"Well, that's interesting," he said, feeling as if he were losing control of the situation.

"It's exciting." She took a sip of her latte, looking across the table at him. "And now you're here."

"I called your mother for a visit when I arrived but she said she wasn't feeling well. You were gone."

Cory's eyes grew wide, and she lowered her mug with a *thunk* on the table. "She didn't want to see you?"

"She said she was sick and that I should come another time. My buddy told me I should have phoned ahead and looking back, I guess that would have been a better idea."

"She said nothing to me." Cory frowned then gave him an apologetic smile. "I'm sorry. I should tell you that Mom isn't that well. She's been struggling with fibromyalgia the past number of years, though it was getting better once we discovered that Matthew had found you."

"So why was she avoiding me?"

Cory bit one corner of her lip as if seeking the right words. "We didn't know you were coming. Matthew had been trying for months to connect with you. We just heard that it might be a possibility, but then, nothing more."

"I was on a trip and out of phone contact. I had some stuff to deal with and I just needed to get away." His beloved foster mother, Rebecca had passed away and he needed some space.

For a moment he was tempted to tell her about his life but part of him held back the information. He wasn't ready yet. He hadn't been there for her when it happened. She was alone in the house Nik had fixed up for her. After all, she'd done for him, she should not have died alone. He should have been there.

Rebecca was the best mother he'd had and now, all he had left was his biological mother and a sister he didn't know who lived in the same town he had.

"Have you lived long in Sweet Creek?" he continued, wondering if the Baleys knew his mother was here. Was that the reason they kept him hidden in the house? Were they afraid they might lose their meal ticket? "You been here all your life?" He couldn't bear to think his natural mother had lived here all along and he had never known.

But Cory shook her head. "No. We moved here for the first time over a year ago. Before that we were... well... were moved all over the place."

Nik sensed a story hung between the hesitations and the vague words, yet relief sluiced through him. It was sheer coincidence Cory and her mother ended up in Sweet Creek.

"Do you need any refills?" Claire's voice broke into his thoughts and he jumped.

"I'm good," he said looking up at her. But her eyes were on Cory, her expression concerned.

"Are you okay?" Claire asked, laying a gentle hand on Cory's shoulder, then lightly rubbing her back.

"Yeah. I'm fine. It's just... my brother is... finally here." Cory's voice broke and he could see the shimmer of tears. "I've thought about you for so many years," she said turning to him as she swiped at her eyes.

"So you always knew about me?" Nik was surprised.

"From the beginning." Her voice held a note of melancholy. "When things got tough, I used to dream you'd come swooping into my life to rescue me."

Things were tough for her?

He wanted to know more, but now was not the time. He had too many things to absorb and think about it.

"Cory and her friend Kelsey had dreams of heroes," Claire said with a chuckle. "I think, at one time, you were hers until Matthew came along."

Matthew. Her fiancé and the lawyer who had contacted him.

"Well, I've never been anyone's hero," he said with a smile.

Claire's bemused look created an unwelcome warmth.

"So, would you be okay with meeting Mom tonight?" Cory asked.

"I guess the question is, would she be okay with meeting me?" Nik replied, dragging his attention back to his sister.

"I'm sure she would. She just needed time to prepare herself."

"Okay. Then I'll see you tonight," Nik said.

Cory nodded and glanced up at Claire. "I'll be a minute or two yet."

"Don't rush. I know you've waited for this moment with Nik for a long time." Claire glanced over at Nik again. "I guess you'll be around for a while now."

The edge in her voice seemed at odds with her smile. He thought again of her reaction when he told her about his deal on the house.

She didn't seem happy about it. At all.

Well, she only had to put up with him for a few months. Then he would be gone.

CHAPTER 2

"You owe me that money, Tom," Claire said, fighting the urge to yell as she turned her car onto the road leading to her parents' place to pick up her dog and daughter. "You know I need it for my down-payment."

Every time she used her hands-free feature in the car, she felt like she had to shout. Her mother always accused her of sounding angry.

Right now, she was. A bit.

"If I don't get it I'll lose my chance to buy my house," she continued, hoping her cousin's lackadaisical heart would be moved by her plea.

"Yeah, well, I know that. I'm waiting for some money, too," he said, heaving out a substantial sigh as if he were even more hard done by the situation than she was.

"Last week you said you'd have the money by tomorrow," Claire said. Then blew out her own frustrated sigh. "I should never have sold you that car. Maybe I should come and take it back."

"Well now, you can't do that," Tom said. "You signed that car over fair and square."

"You not paying me is hardly fair and square."

"If you need the money so bad, why don't you borrow it from your mom and dad?"

Claire clenched her hands on the steering wheel of her car, wishing Tom was right in front of her so she could pinch him like she used to whenever he annoyed her. Though right now what he needed was far more than a pinch. More like a punch.

"There's no way I'm asking my mom and dad to borrow any money," Claire said. "Not when my cousin is the one who owes me $8000."

As if she would go to her parents for the money, anyway.

Claire remembered too well the financial feuds her mother and father went through after they moved to this large, expensive home on its large, expensive lot. It seemed like they fought every night.

Though things were better now, money was still tight, much to her mother's chagrin and her father's frustration.

"When is the earliest you can pay me?" Claire asked, pretending she hadn't heard all his excuses.

"I'll talk to a guy who owes me the money," Tom said. "I'll tell him I need it quicker."

"Give me a date," Claire insisted.

"I'll call you tomorrow," Tom said. And Claire knew that was all she was getting out of him.

She said goodbye, then called up Devon's number. While her hands-free system dialed, she pulled a long, slow and steady breath.

She wasn't above asking God to help her out on this. She knew she would need divine intervention for everything to come together. Devon had never been keen on the agreement Claire had signed with Mrs. Blatchford. And since getting power of attorney over affairs after her stroke, he had let Claire know loud and clear what he thought of their deal.

Not much.

"Hey Claire," Devon said, sounding extra cheery.

"How's your mom doing?" she asked. Claire had meant to visit the past couple of months, but life had gotten busy and Calgary wasn't around the corner.

"She's doing okay, though it will be a long haul before she's back to normal."

"I'm sorry to hear that," Claire said. She paused a few seconds, deciding how to move on to the next topic without sounding hardhearted.

"I'm guessing you're phoning about your agreement with my mother," Devon said, thankfully bringing up the topic for her.

"You're exactly right." Claire slowed as she turned down her parents' driveway, glancing at the clock on the dashboard. She was cutting things close making phone calls on her way to pick up Emma, but once she got her daughter, she couldn't have these discussions in front of her. She needed this done as soon as possible.

"What can I do for you?"

Claire bit her lip, realizing that she would be making the same excuses her cousin Tom had just made to her.

"I was wondering if I could ask for an extension," she said, disliking how desperate she sounded. Too much was on the line for her and she wished it didn't matter as much as it did. It was hard enough finding a reasonably priced house that she could afford in Sweet Creek. But this wasn't just any ordinary house, this was her old home. The place she wanted so badly for Emma. The home she hoped to create for her daughter.

And Nik would destroy it if he got it.

The silence that followed her request wasn't encouraging.

"I know we said I had to come up with the money in the next week," she continued, hoping he was thinking instead of waiting to find a way to say no. "But I am waiting for my cousin to pay me for the car I sold him. I've got two thirds of the down payment together already and once I get that money from him I'll have it all." She tightened her grip on the steering wheel, sending up another silent prayer.

"I should tell you I have another offer on the house," Devon said. "It's higher than yours, so I don't have much incentive to give you a break."

He sounded so reasonable, but behind his words she heard a faint reprimand. Devon knew Claire and his mother were the ones who had agreed on the price. Claire also knew Devon had told his mother it wasn't enough money. But Mrs. Blatchford insisted, reminding Devon that it was Claire's childhood home.

"I have a deal with your mother," Claire said.

"And I'm honoring that deal," Devon said. "So you don't have to worry about that. Now I just need you to honor your end of it and we'll be okay."

Claire pulled up beside her mother's small car, fighting the panic tightening her chest as she tried to think of something to convince Devon to give her some time. But she drew a blank.

"Okay. I'll get it done. Give my greetings to your mother. I hope to come and visit her in the next couple of weeks."

"That would be nice," he said. He then said goodbye and hung up. The dial tone echoed in the car.

Claire turned the engine off and dragged in a long, slow breath as an ache began at the base of her neck. She had no choice. She had to trust that Tom would pay what he owed her.

She thought of Emma playing on that swing set, constantly talking about the bedroom in the house that would be hers once they bought it. This was her childhood home. Claire had a much stronger stake in it than Nik did, who, according to him, only saw it as a business opportunity.

Besides, the house was perfectly situated between her parents' place and the school. Once Emma was older, she could walk to school. It was close to Claire's work; it had a large yard with lots of space for Emma to play in.

Ever since she and her parents had moved to this place, Claire missed her old home with its unique cubbies, hidey-holes and the awkward closets her mother always complained about.

She loved the huge, open kitchen that looked out over the yard. But most of all, she loved the deep, oversized bay window in the dining room. On rainy days she would drag her blanket and book and sit on the window seat, curled up to read and watch the rain falling on the yard.

The other reason she wanted the home had more to do with her well-meaning mother dropping vague hints about how different Emma's childhood was from Claire's. Living in an apartment, there was no decent yard to play in. Her mother meant to be sympathetic, but it came across as patronizing and judgmental.

Claire tried not to state the obvious — that she was a single mom doing her best. By purchasing second-hand clothing, eating at home, taking Emma places that cost nothing, driving an old beater of a car and living in a crappy but cheap apartment, she'd pulled together most of the down payment herself. Something she was proud of. When she got

Andy's sports car after he died, she saw it as divine intervention. She could sell it and get the rest.

But now it looked like the dream she had worked so hard and made so many sacrifices for was slipping from her hands.

Panic gripped her heart with an icy fist. She couldn't spend another winter in that drafty apartment. Shivering each morning as she prepared her daughter's lunch. Struggling with drains that would plug, pipes that would leak and that smell her daughter hated so much slowly getting worse. Spending another Thanksgiving and another Christmas in that apartment was too depressing to contemplate.

All summer she'd imagined Christmas in the house. A large spruce tree with twinkling lights in the living room, a fire snapping in the hearth, music on the stereo and garlands of greenery snaking up the wooden bannister to the upstairs bedrooms.

And the smell of gingerbread cookies baking in an oven that worked. To think of that all being taken away was heart-rending.

It doesn't have to happen.

A thought snaked around the edges of her mind.

It's eight-thousand dollars. Surely, by now, your parents could help you?

But she had never asked for their help and it had been a point of pride. Ever since she had given them the news that she was pregnant — that she and Andy decided to get married to give their child a home — she had keenly felt their disappointment.

She had always been the good girl. The one who did everything right. Not like her sister, Tess, who had tossed aside a great career opportunity, broke up with her fiancé and taken off to Europe.

Claire was the hope of the Kruger family. She was a scholar headed for a law degree and a bright future.

Then she got pregnant.

And after Emma was born, Andy left her. While her mother hadn't said anything at the time, Claire keenly felt her mother's disappointed shame. As well, her relief was that none of this happened in Sweet Creek.

As a result, when Claire moved back here, she was determined to show her parents and the rest of Sweet Creek that she could give Emma a good life.

And that she could give her a decent home.

Claire shook off the negative thoughts, stepping inside the house to the sound of her daughter's laughter and the scent of baking. *Making cookies again,* Claire thought, knowing her mother would send half of the batch home with her and Emma.

She toed her shoes off and set them on the rack inside the foyer of the house. Following the spicy scent of cookies, she walked through the large high-ceilinged living room with its metallic gas fireplace and white furniture. She stepped up the two stairs into the kitchen. Emma sat on the granite island, frowning, her tongue clamped between her lips as she concentrated on piping some icing onto a cookie. Her hair was neatly braided, and she wore an oversized apron covered with smears of flour. Claire's mother looked up as Claire came into the kitchen, flashing her a smile.

"Can you wait a moment? We just have to finish up," she said.

Claire tossed her purse on a chair and then came to join them. "Gingerbread men. Already?"

"We're practicing for Christmas," Emma said.

"That's three months away."

"Emma wanted to make gingerbread men," her mother said.

"Well, those look amazing," she said. "Can I have one?"

Emma didn't even look at her, still focused on what she was doing. "Don't take too many," she said. "Grandpa asked us to save some for him."

Claire looked at the dozens of gingerbread men spread out over the counter and guessed there would be lots for her father to eat. She took one that looked like a practice cookie and bit off one lopsided leg. It was still warm, and it made her realize how hungry she was. In spite of the down-time when Nik had come to the coffee shop, the rest of Claire's day had been too busy to even grab lunch. And no chance to talk to Cory about her reaction to having her brother around.

"Are you almost done?" Claire asked, glancing at her watch. "We need to get home on time so I can make supper."

"I don't want to go back to the apartment," Emma grumped, as she finished up her cookie. "It smells bad and it's dark."

Claire ignored her mother's concerned look. She wasn't sure what had caused the smell Emma was referring to. The landlord knew of the stink; she had told him enough times. But it had only gotten worse. Nor could she do anything about the small windows that let in precious little light.

Her thoughts shifted to her old house with its large south-facing windows. She remembered playing in the sunbeams, warming herself in the sun. Again, she stifled a flash of fear at the thought that Emma might not have the chance to make the same memories. She had a righteous claim to that house, and she had to make sure it happened.

Emma turned to her grandmother. "Can we stay here tonight?"

Deborah gave Emma an apologetic look. "I'd love that, but I have company coming tonight so there won't be any room. Your great uncle Steven and his whole family will be staying here."

Her mother sighed as she glanced at Claire. "It's not really a good time, but they are between moves and they asked and what could I say? He's my brother."

"You don't need to apologize to me about that," Claire said. "I certainly didn't figure on staying here."

"But I did. I just don't like that smell," Emma grumbled.

"Sorry honey," Claire said, gently smoothing a wisp of hair back from her daughter's forehead. "I will talk to Mr. Landlord about the smell again.

I'm sure it's just something in one of the other apartments."

"It's really yucky," Emma said, looking at her grandmother as if she had a solution to the problem.

"Mr. Landlord hasn't been very cooperative," her mother said with a sniffy tone. "I sure wish you could just move out of there now."

"Working on that." Claire fought down a shiver of panic.

"When will you know if the house is yours?"

As if it were a foregone conclusion.

"I have until Monday to meet the conditions. And I can't until cousin Tom pays me for the car."

"You sold that car to him weeks ago."

"Five to be precise." Claire took another bite of her cookie, for a moment wishing it was Tom's arm she was taking off. Such viciousness!

"You should take it back and sell it again."

"I should." Claire inspected the cookie, trying to figure out what part to eat next. "But I signed it over to him. He's the legal owner of the car."

She tried to ignore her mother's eye roll. She knew she had been negligent, but she had trusted Tom. If you couldn't trust family, who could you?

"Have you spoken to Mrs. Blatchford about extending the agreement?"

"I can't. She had a stroke, remember? Her son has Power of Attorney over her estate and he's the one I dealt with."

"You should never have sold that car to Tom. I know his father often despairs of that boy ever turning his life around. I thought things were going well, but they're not. I can't believe you assumed he was dependable enough to purchase your car. As for Devon, I think he should give you some more time. After all, it's not your fault Tom is so untrustworthy. Besides, you have wanted that house for so long."

And here we go, Claire thought fighting her annoyance as her mother kept talking. If she didn't distract her mother, she would keep going and eventually return to Claire's lack of judgement. And with that, the unspoken negatives on Claire's current situation.

"Apparently there's another buyer," she said, the comment bursting out of her. "And he offered more than I did."

"Who?"

Claire looked over at Emma, her lips pursed in concentration as she iced the next cookie.

Claire lowered her voice. "Nik Austin. He's Cory's long-lost brother and Joyce's long-lost son."

Her mother's wide eyes told Claire she had shifted her mother's focus.

"The one she gave up for adoption?" Deborah asked.

Claire patted the air between them, signing to her mother to lower her voice.

"Yes. That one. The only one. And he's back in town to connect with them."

"And he's buying that house out from under you?"

Claire made another shushing motion, glancing at Emma, but her daughter's tongue was out, and she was frowning. A sure sign she wasn't listening.

"It's not a done deal," Claire said, easing out a sigh. "Not until Monday."

"Do you have any other options?" her mother asked.

Claire looked around her parent's house, a thought teasing her. Did she dare ask? Was it worth putting up with a few more eye rolls and some condescension to give her daughter the home she always wanted to?

Please, Lord, she prayed, show me what to do? I'm scared.

As she prayed she wished the panic that was circling would ease off.

Ask your mother. Just ask.

She took another deep breath, sent up another prayer and was about to speak when the shrill ring of the phone cut her off.

Her mother glanced at call display while the phone sent out its insistent demands and let it ring.

"You're not answering it?" Claire asked, puzzled at her mother's actions. As long as she could remember, her mother never, ever let the phone ring. Wasn't polite, she told them. Besides, her mother's innate curiosity needed to be satiated. She always answered.

"It's the bank. Your father can deal with them." Her mother flapped her hand in a dismissive gesture.

"What does the bank want?"

Her mother heavily sighed. "It's fine. Just some… well… bookkeeping things we need to take care of."

"Is everything okay with the store?"

"The store is doing well."

"And you guys?"

Her mother's mouth became a prim line as she tucked a strand of hair behind her ear. "We'll be fine. We just need to get through this… this thing."

Claire felt a niggling dread, guessing "this thing" had everything to do with her parents' finances and how they had overextended themselves building their house.

While she felt bad for her parents, she also realized there was no way she could approach them about a temporary loan to buy the house.

Don't panic. Relax. Tom said he was getting the money together.

She had to believe that.

Emma finished the cookie she had been decorating, but she took her sweet time taking her apron off and washing her hands. Claire tried not to fuss or hurry her along, because she knew that would only make her daughter move slower.

"Is Mooch in the backyard?" Claire asked, walking to the French doors.

"He had a lot of fun playing there," Emma said drying her hands on the towel her grandmother gave her. "I don't think he likes it in the apartment, either."

Claire fully agreed with Emma. When her parents had given Emma a dog for her birthday that spring, Claire tried to explain this to them. She was working, she didn't have time to take care of a dog, nor did they have a suitable place for him. But her mother had reiterated the fact that come fall Claire would live in the house next door. With a great big yard. Mooch would have lots of room to play then and she agreed to watch Mooch at their place until then.

"I'll get Mooch if you can get Emma ready to go," Claire said to her mother, opening the door and calling for the dog. He was stretched out on the lawn beside the swing set, snoozing in the warm sun. He lifted his head then lowered it again, as if hoping Claire would forget about him. He was as unwilling to leave as Emma was.

Ten minutes later Claire had her reluctant passengers in the car and with a final farewell to her mother, she drove away.

"Can we get pizza for supper?" Emma asked as they drove back through town to get home.

"No. I have chicken out and I thought we could have potatoes and beans with it."

"I hate 'tatos," Emma grumbled.

"Please don't say that," Claire said, reprimanding her daughter. "You're lucky to have such good food to eat." And she got the potatoes from Tess, who got them at the Farmer's Market she worked at from time to time.

"Gramma said we could have supper with her," Emma said. "That would be good food too and her house smells nice. And Mooch would have room to play."

"Maybe Mooch should stay at Gramma's all the time," Claire muttered.

"No, he's my dog," Emma said, hugging him tight, as if Claire would take him away any minute.

"I know he is, honey. And he's a good dog. He just needs more room than we have." Claire suppressed yet another sigh as they pulled into the parking spot behind the apartment. Claire compared the dingy building with its broken and taped-up windows, its missing siding, to her parent's immaculate home.

As she always did when she parked by the apartment she glanced at the house beside it, counting down the time.

Once again, she pushed down the flutter of panic that her dream was dying and, grabbing Mooch's leash, stepped out of the car. But Emma was already unbuckled and opening the door on her side.

"Honey, wait until I can get Mooch," Claire warned.

But it was too late. The door was open and Mooch saw his opportunity. He scrambled past Emma and shot out of the open door.

"Mooch. Get back here," Claire yelled, hurrying around the front of the car to catch him.

He didn't listen and instead scooted through the opening in the fence before Claire could stop him.

"Mommy, you have to get Mooch before that man gets him," Emma called out.

"I know. I know." Claire knelt at the opening of the fence looking through. Of course, Mooch headed right for the flower beds he had dug in before. Claire suspected he had buried a bone there some time over the summer and was determined to get it now.

"Mooch. Come here," she called, unwilling to go through the fence in case Nik was home. But the dog wouldn't come. Pushing down a beat of frustration she squeezed herself through the hole and ran over to Mooch, who was now spraying dirt behind him, his paws a blur.

She grabbed him by his collar, pulling back on him. "Mooch, stop," she grunted as the dog lunged toward the flower bed again.

"Is he okay, Mommy?" Emma called out from the fence.

"He's fine," Claire said looking with dismay at the hole he had made and the white lily bulbs he had dug up. "I wish I could say the same about this flower bed."

Emma slipped into the yard and ran over to Mooch's side, hugging him again.

"Honey, don't do that, please," Claire said, pulling Mooch away from her daughter. "He'll think you're rewarding his bad behavior."

"But I think he feels bad," Emma said, pouting her displeasure at her mother's reprimand.

Claire doubted that. Mooch was lunging at the flower bed again, ignoring her.

"Really? Again?"

The frustrated voice behind her made Claire's heart plunge. Nik was home after all.

She turned to apologize and felt even worse when she saw his angry expression. Which made her wonder how he felt about his visit with Cory this afternoon.

"I'm sorry. He got out of the car before I could stop him," she said, trying not to sound too apologetic. After all, when she took ownership of the house, the flower garden would be her problem.

Nik glanced from Mooch to Emma, a fleeting glimpse of distress crossing his face. Then, as quickly as it came, it was replaced by a stern frown as he caught sight of the bulbs and dirt scattered on the lawn.

"Again, I apologize. I'll come after supper and clean it up," Claire said, feeling she should make restitution. After all, he *was* living there at the moment, no matter what her deal with Mrs. Blatchford was.

"That's okay." He waved off her offer. "I'm getting great at this."

"Why don't you like my dog?" Emma asked.

This seemed to take Nik by surprise.

"Well, it's not that I don't like your dog," Nik replied, looking rather disconcerted. "It's just I don't like him digging in the flower beds."

Emma seemed to consider this then waggled her head. "Okay. I understand. I will be more careful with him. So he doesn't do it again." She shook her head as she patted Mooch on the head. "You silly dog. You shouldn't make a mess of Mr., um..." She looked at Nik, frowning. "What's your name again?"

"Nik Austin."

"Okay. Mr. Nik Austin's flower beds," Emma said. She tilted her head to one side, as if studying him. "How long will you live here?" she asked.

"Why?"

"Because my mom and I will be moving in. When Mrs. Blatchford sells us the house."

Now it was Nik's turn to frown. "What?" His

gaze flicked to Claire. “What is she talking about?”

“Mrs. Blatchford and my mom,” Emma put in before Claire could find the right words to explain what Emma was talking about. “I’m going to sleep in that room, there.” Emma pointed to one of the gabled windows. “I will paint it pink, like my Aunty Tess painted her room when she lived there. It had princesses in it. Gramma said I can have the bed when I move into the house. My mommy used to live in this house and she love, love, loves it. So do I. It’s a happy house.”

Nik turned to Claire. “Are you the one who has the Offer to Purchase in place right now?”

“Yes. I am.”

Nik’s expression shifted, and he took a step back.

“I have a week to finalize the deal,” Claire said, a defensive tone creeping into her voice.

“Five days, actually,” Nik corrected.

His comment annoyed her. “Whatever. I’m sorry to say I’ll get the money together one way or the other.”

He angled her a skeptical frown. "You look like you don't believe me."

"It's not me. It's Devon who doesn't think you'll manage it."

And now she was really annoyed. Why was Devon talking about her to Nik? He had no right.

But instead of saying more she turned to Emma. "We have to go and have supper," she said. "I'm sure Mr. Nik doesn't want Mooch hanging around causing any more problems."

Emma grimaced, showing Claire what she thought of Claire's command.

"Now, please?" Claire said.

"I have an idea," Emma said, clapping her hands together. "Why don't we make supper and bring it over to Mr. Nik's place? We can eat in the house. That way we don't have to smell that awful smell." She tossed a grin Nik's way, suddenly full of charm and warmth. "Our apartment has a bad smell and Mr. Landlord won't fix it. It makes me want to barf whenever we eat."

"Emma," Claire said, shocked at her daughter's forthright and rude comment. "We don't talk like that."

"But I do talk like that," she said, innocence personified.

"You shouldn't and you know better." Claire put her free hand on her daughter's shoulder, steering her toward the hole in the fence. "And now we need to leave."

Emma pulled a grumpy face then waved to

Nik. "Goodbye, Mr. Nik, maybe we can visit another time."

But Nik just stared at them, looking confused. As if he wasn't sure what to make of Emma's sudden switch in allegiance.

Claire wasn't either. But for now, she had supper to make and a list longer than her arm of things to do before the sun came up again.

So she said goodbye and took the dog and Emma back to their place through the fence.

* * *

NIK SLID his damp palms down the side of his blue jeans as he stood by his truck.

All these years of wondering. Of not knowing who his mother was or why she had done what she had were coming to a close.

Would Joyce tell him everything? Would she explain?

Rebecca would have told him to pray. To forgive. There were many times she would comfort him when he cried, wondering why his mother had given him up. Wondering why the Jensen's didn't want him anymore. Why the Baleys were so cruel. So many questions she couldn't answer.

So she would pray with him, reminding him that God's love was a faithful love.

Still, he hesitated.

The easiest thing would be to leave. To walk away from the questions and the pain.

But he knew they would follow him. He needed to face them once and for all. Hopefully, talking to his mother could give him some answers.

And when he tore down that house he could eradicate the pain the Baleys had inflicted on him and finally put that part of his life behind him.

Maybe coming to Sweet Creek was just what he needed to do. Maybe, when he left, he could find the peace that had eluded him for so long.

Despite his self-talk, his heart pounded like he had just run a marathon. He clenched and unclenched his fists, drew in a long, slow breath and strode up the sidewalk to the apartment before he could change his mind.

He was disappointed to see his fingers shake as he punched in the numbers Cory had given him on the keypad.

"It's me, Nik," he said when Cory's voice came through the intercom.

"I'll let you in. Just open the door when you

hear the buzzer," she said, her voice distant. Reserved.

He paused for a moment, second thoughts assailing him but when the door buzzed, he yanked it open and strode through.

Nik walked down a long, narrow hallway, checking the numbers as he went. A door at the end of the hallway opened and Cory stood there, smiling.

But as he drew near, he could see that her smile seemed tight and her eyes held a glint of concern.

"Everything okay?" he asked as he came near.

She glanced back over her shoulder into the apartment. "Mom's nervous, that's all. How about you?"

"Ditto. But we're still okay, right?"

Her careful smile struck him as hesitant.

Maybe this wasn't such a good idea.

Nik shoved his hands in the back pocket of his jeans, trying to still the trembling of his hands. He did nothing, waiting for Cory to make the next move; to let him know what to do.

After what seemed like eons but was probably only seconds, she indicated that he follow her inside. He pulled in another breath as years of questions, doubts and tears trailed behind him like a dark cloud. His step faltered when he saw the woman sitting in the recliner facing him.

"Mom, Nik is here," Cory said, her voice quiet.

Nik stopped and all he could do was stare.

All his life, whenever he thought of his mother, he pulled out the hazy memory he had of her wearing blue jeans and a sweatshirt, carrying him, holding him tight, her long hair brushing his face.

The next memory was of her leaving, walking out of the door of a large, white room, filled with other people, the hood of her sweatshirt covering her head. He had tried to run after her but he was pulled back.

This woman was nothing like that. This woman looked old. Tired. Wrinkles fanned out from her eyes, and two deep lines bracketed her mouth. Her hair was short and hung in a grey bob framing her face.

His first emotion was disappointment.

But as she looked up at him, her brown eyes so much like his, so much like Cory's, filled with tears. She struggled to her feet, wincing in pain.

"Nik. My son," she said, her voice thick with emotion as she came toward him.

He had rehearsed this moment so many times. Thought of it so often. Sometimes he ran to her, wrapped his arms around her and cried on her shoulder.

Others he simply looked at her, told her she'd had her chance and walked away.

But this wasn't his imagination—it was reality. And all he could do was freeze and stare at this woman trying to reconcile past with present.

"I'm so sorry," was all she said, blinking rapidly, tears drifting down her cheeks.

Move. Do something.

But he couldn't.

Finally, Joyce lowered her hand but Nik saw the anguish on her face.

"I made some coffee," Cory said. "Why don't we sit down and have a cup?"

Nik blinked, trying to pull himself into the moment, wondering why he could look at this woman who was his mother and not feel something at her apology. In all the movies and television shows this was where the violins came in, sweet and sweeping, and people embraced and held each other close, reunited at last.

But this woman created none of those emotions in him.

What kind of monster was he that he couldn't even hug his own mother? And, even worse, as he sat down the only person he could think about was Rebecca. The woman who had poured unconditional love into him and who had taught him of God's love. Who had prayed with him and comforted him.

"Just sit wherever," Cory said. "I'll be right back."

Nik nodded, then eased himself onto a worn couch across from Joyce. His mother, he corrected himself.

"So, how long have you lived here?" he asked, resting his hands on his knee. Thank goodness it wasn't jittering. Yet.

"About a year now," Joyce said, her eyes fixed on him. "Cory and I moved around a lot before we ended up here."

"I see," was all he could say. Silence followed his comment and he glanced to the kitchen, hoping Cory would appear soon. He had felt more comfortable with her around.

He scanned the living room, his eyes skittering over the few plants and knick-knacks set out on the bookshelf on one wall. He came to an abrupt stop, having caught sight of a picture. He walked over to it, picking the framed photo up.

A toddler laughed at the photographer, tucked in the arms of a young woman. Joyce in better years, Nik guessed.

"That's you. When you were three," Joyce said from her chair. "Your father took that picture."

"I have a father?" Matthew had said nothing about a father when they finally connected.

"Had. He died a week after that picture was taken."

"I see." His hands clutched at the photo, a storm of varying emotions washing over him. He'd had a father. At one time, he'd had a father and a mother. A complete family.

"He was very proud of you and was so excited to be a dad," Joyce continued, her comments only stirring up the uncertain feelings.

"What... what happened to him?" Nik asked, swallowing a knot of pain, surprised that this revelation generated such feelings.

"He was hit by a truck as he was walking home from work. Never found the driver."

"Do you have any photos of him?"

"There's an album on the coffee table," Cory said.

Nik turned as Cory spoke. She was carrying a tray holding two mugs and a plate of cookies, which she set on the table, then picked up a red album the word 'Photos' barely illegibly engraved on its cracked and worn surface.

Nik remembered a time when he lived with

the Baley family. They had gone to a park and he had wanted to somersault down the hill. Rick Baley had warned him not to but he did anyhow. He could still recall the feeling of disorientation and movement beyond his control as he tumbled down the hill end over end.

That's how felt now.

He took the album from Cory. For a moment he just held it, running his finger along the cracked edge. Should he open it and be shown what he had lost when his mother gave him up?

Finally, he turned the page and the first thing he saw was a wedding picture. Joyce and…

"What was his name?" he asked.

"Taylor," Joyce said. "Taylor Luciuk."

Nik stared at the young couple, his eyes shifting from Joyce to Taylor. His mother and his father.

"You look exactly like him," Cory said.

Nik studied him closer. "I guess I do."

Nik flipped another page and his eyes fixed on another photo of a man holding a baby.

"That's Dad and you," Cory said, pointing to it.

Nik struggled to quiet his pounding heart. Find his footing.

He looked over at Joyce, then down at the picture. His family. The one he lost.

"And what about your adoptive parents?" Cory asked. "Where do they live? Are they still alive?"

Nik held her gaze, wondering for a fleeting second if she was mocking him. Then he realized they had no clue about the Jensen's.".

"Mom and Dad... Audry and Karl," he corrected, still struggling with the sting, "got divorced three and half years after they adopted me. I went into the foster system after that."

"Oh, no," Cory cried out. Her distress was obvious as was the look of shock on her face. "I can't believe that… Mom was assured you would be taken care of. She was convinced you were in a good place. That's so heartbreaking…" her voice trailed off.

Her reaction surprised him. What had happened to him was such a part of his story it seemed as if everyone who knew him knew of it. Rebecca did, his friends did, even his ex-girlfriend did.

Now, here he was with his closest family members and they had no clue.

"You were in foster care?" Joyce cried out. "Why did no one tell me?"

"It was a closed adoption," Nik said. He

couldn't keep the bitter tone out of his voice. "You wanted nothing to do with me."

"That's not true," Joyce exclaimed, leaning forward and reaching out with one hand as if to connect with him. "That's what the social worker recommended. And I didn't want to mess things up for you. I didn't want to get in the way of your new parents."

"Your adoptive parents divorced?" Cory asked, as if she still couldn't understand.

"Looking back, I think they were having troubles before they adopted me. I think they were hoping having me would change things, but they only made their situation worse."

"Were you ever happy?" Joyce pleaded.

Nik hesitated, not sure what to say. He held Joyce's anguished gaze and saw more tears spill down her cheeks. For a moment he felt sorry for her.

"I was happy for a while," he said. "But my adoptive parents fought a lot. I spent a lot of time by myself in my room playing with all the toys they bought me."

"You said you went into foster care after that," Cory said, laying her hand on his arm. "What was that like?"

"Terrible." Nik clenched his hands into fists,

struggling to keep his emotions in check. It was that house, he thought. It was being back in that house that brought back all the wrong memories.

Cory covered her mouth with her hand, crying as well.

"I'm so sorry," she whispered. "We never knew. We had no idea."

"You were supposed to be safe. You were supposed to be in a good place," Joyce cried out. "I was told it was the best solution."

Nik looked down at the album, at the different pictures pasted in it, glimpses of the life that he had before everything fell apart. His knee started jittering, shaking, bouncing up and down.

Then Joyce got up, crying, walking down the hall. The door shut behind her and Nik felt the breath he'd held slip out of him.

His mother was leaving him again.

He looked at the mugs of coffee Cory had poured, wondering what to do. His body hummed with a mixture of anger and pain.

He stood, setting the album on the table. "I'm sorry," he stammered. "I have to leave, too."

"But you just got here," Cory said, getting up as well.

"I know. And I apologize," he said, running his palms up and down his thighs. "Thanks for having me." The words sounded hollow and small.

He walked out the door, Cory right behind, keeping step with him as they walked down the carpeted hall. When they came to the door leading outside, he stopped and turned to her. "So I don't think that went particularly well."

"I understand. We knew this would be hard for you but I had hoped my mother would be a little more understanding."

Nik looked into her eyes, struggling again with his emotions.

"Are you okay?" she asked.

He sighed, not sure how to encapsulate all the feelings storming through him.

"Yeah. I'm okay."

Cory gave him a tremulous smile, and then he gave her what he couldn't give his mother. A tight hug.

She clung to him for a moment, then pulled away, swiping at her eyes. "So how long you sticking around?"

"Well, if it's any consolation, I put an offer in on a house."

Cory's mouth eased into a smile and Nik saw her relax. "So you'll be staying?"

"For a while," was all Nik would tell her.

"I'm glad to hear that," she said. She reached out and gave his shoulder a squeeze. "I know this evening didn't go the way we all hoped it would, but like you said, it's a start, right?"

"You're right," Nik agreed.

"I'm glad you came," Cory said. "Let me know when you want to come again."

"I'll be back," Nik promised her. "I need to sort a few things out first."

Cory nodded. "Of course. I understand. There's a lot to process. I think I was being romantic when I hoped we would all fall into each other's arms and be one big happy family."

Nik gave her a wry smile. "To be honest, I hoped for the same."

She returned his smile and walked with him as he went through the front doors. She stayed on the step with her arms folded over her chest, watching Nik get in his truck.

Nik backed out of the parking lot and glanced over to see Cory waving to him. The sight warmed his heart.

But as he left, he knew it would take a few days before he would see his mother again.

He just needed time.

CHAPTER 3

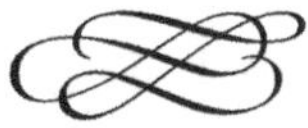

"Is Mr. Nik going camping?" Emma stood on a chair with her nose pressed against the window, looking out over the Blatchford yard.

"What do you mean?" Claire asked as she finished loading the dishwasher. She turned it on and joined her daughter. Supper was over and soon the usual bed-time battle she'd been having lately with Emma would begin.

"He has a camper. Like my friend, Lacy's mom and dad do. Lacy says they go camping every year. She says they bring it to their yard every time they go. So they can load it up." She frowned as she saw a medium-sized holiday trailer being backed into the yard, guided by Nik's truck.

"I have no idea what he's up to," Claire said, but the sight ratcheted her unease.

Yesterday, late in the afternoon, Tom had stopped by Coffee Creek with a post-dated check for her. Claire had almost given up on him, but she was thankful he had finally fulfilled his end of the deal. By the time she was finished at work, the bank was closed. So she deposited the check in the night deposit box, hoping it would go into her account today or Monday at the latest.

She had phoned Devon to update him but she was put through to his answering machine.

Claire was fully aware of the ticking clock, and the panic that gripped her tighter every day. When she came back from work, she looked at her bank balance but the check was not in yet. She wouldn't relax until that check cleared, realizing she was cutting things close.

But now it looked like her neighbor was setting up camp, following through on his potential plans. Did he know something she didn't?

Well, he would just have to move it on Monday, she told herself.

"I wish we could go camping," Emma said, a wistful note in her voice.

"I wish we could go, too," Claire said, empathizing with her, remembering trips to the lake she and Tess made with their parents. Trips that they'd quit once they moved to the new house.

"If I had a dad, could we go camping then?" Emma asked, looking up at her. "Lacy says we don't go camping because I don't have a dad."

Lacy was becoming a pain, Claire thought.

"We don't go camping because we don't have a tent or a trailer and right now Mommy is too busy—"

"With Coffee Creek. I know." Emma released the last two words on a gusty sigh. "I wish you weren't so busy. I wish we could do more stuff together."

"I know, honey." Claire brushed her hand over Emma's unruly curls, the usual stab of guilt slicing at her gut. The plight of a single mom. Too much to do and only so much of her to go around. She glanced over at the house, unease prickling her spine. If they bought the house, it would mean less money to do what they wanted.

But it would give them a home, space for Emma to play and that was important, too. Wasn't it?

"At any rate Missy, it's almost time for bed," Claire said, forcing aside the questions. She had gone over the pros and cons of buying the house so many times she could probably recite them backwards. No matter how often she went over the list, the pros had always outweighed the cons. A home for her daughter. Security for them. Equity building up. "Brush your teeth and pick out a book and I'll meet you in your bedroom."

Mooch stood by the door whining, scratching on the rug.

"I think Mooch needs to go outside," Emma said. "Can I take him? I haven't played much with him today."

"You played with him at Grammas."

"No. I didn't. Gramma said I had to give Uncle Bill's little boy and girl a chance to play with him."

Claire's aunt and uncle arrived the day before, filling the house with their laughter and boisterous children. Claire wondered how her mother would cope with the noise and the busyness.

"Okay then, but only for ten minutes," Claire warned. That would give her enough time to tidy up. "And make sure he doesn't go through the fence."

Emma grabbed Mooch's ball and leash, clipping it onto his collar and took him out the door. Claire watched out the window as they entered the backyard of the apartment. Emma tossed the ball, standing by the opening to the other yard, guarding it.

Satisfied they wouldn't be bothering Nik, Claire returned to washing the dishes. The dishwasher had broken down, of course, so she was stuck doing dishes by hand.

She filled the sink and poured the soap into the water when she smelled something. It wasn't the usual smell that Emma always complained about. This was stronger. Harsher.

Puzzled she walked to the window. Was someone burning something outside?

She looked onto the yard.

Mooch was tied up to the fence, but Emma was nowhere to be seen.

That stinker. Claire was about to head out the door when she remembered the water filling the sink.

She ran into the kitchen, her heart sinking. Too late. The water poured from the small sink and pooled all over the floor. Of course. Of course. Claire hurried over to turn off the taps just as the smoke detector squealed, hurting her ears.

What in the world?

She spun around and slipped on the soapy water.

Her ankle twisted as she fell. Pain shot through her leg, debilitating her. She couldn't move but she had to. She had to get out of there.

* * *

"ARE YOU GOING CAMPING?"

Nik spun around, looking to see where the voice came from.

Then he saw Emma crouched down, looking through the hole in the fence.

"No. I'm just moving my trailer here." He was finished blocking it up, and it was all levelled. All he had to do was hook up the power.

"Will you leave it there when my mommy buys the house?" Emma asked.

Nik chewed his lip, trying to figure out how to answer this. This morning he had called Devon to discover the status of Claire's claim on the house. Devon had told him he hadn't received his money from Claire yet, so unless a miracle occurred by Monday, their deal still held. He would have left his trailer where it was, but the owner of the lot had called to tell him he had to get it out of there or incur additional fees to continue holding it on the lot.

As he held Emma's hopeful gaze, though, he

refused to be the one to shatter her dream. So, he gave her a tentative smile, meanwhile scrambling for words that would satisfy and, hopefully let her down gently.

"I'll have to find another place for it, then, won't I?" It was the best he could come up with as those soft blue eyes stared up at him.

"I've never been in a camper before," Emma told him, rocking back and forth, toe to heel, the sun glistening off her unruly hair. "Can I come and look inside?"

Her audacity made him grin. This kid would go far based on her sheer determination and push.

"I'll just look in the door," she continued, seeming to take his silence for a subtle giving in. "I won't go right inside and snoop around. Just poke my head in."

"I don't think your mother would want you coming onto the yard, let alone looking in my camper." Because that didn't sound creepy at all.

Emma scrunched up her face, as if thinking. "Maybe not. But I would take a quick peek. I tied Mooch up so he won't come on the yard."

Nik had to chuckle. This girl had an irresistible charm. And as he listened to her, he felt a softening in his heart. An emptiness that had always lurked as if waiting for the right person to fill it.

She's not your child.

He shook off the emotions, reality intruding with the practical voice. And yet he found himself drawn to this little girl.

"Please," she asked. "Just a few seconds of your time?"

Again he had to laugh. "You'd make an excellent salesperson," he said.

"That's what my grandpa always says. He told me that when I'm old enough I can come and work in the hardware store. Or be a lawyer."

"Okay, you can have a look, but please don't go inside."

"Yay." Emma fist pumped then skipped toward the trailer. "Where do you go camping with your trailer?"

"I don't. I mostly use it when..." he hesitated, still not sure how to tell her what he hoped to do with the house. "...when I need another place to stay."

"My mommy said it's hard to find a place in Sweet Creek because there aren't enough 'partments for all the people, so you can live in your trailer when me and mommy move into the house."

Again Nik was at a loss for words. According to Devon, Claire couldn't meet the conditions to purchase the property. Nik wasn't sure how Devon knew but the clock was ticking down to Monday. And this little girl seemed to think they were moving into the house. He wished he knew how to tell her it might not happen. But, again, that wasn't his responsibility.

"Is this where I go in?" Emma asked, pointing to the steps he had just put down.

"Yes. Let me get the door for you, it's hard to open."

He reached past her and as he did, he heard a shrill buzzing coming from behind him, then another and another.

They were coming from Emma's and her mother's apartment.

"What is that?" Emma asked, frowning as she looked over her shoulder.

He caught the whiff of something burning the same time he saw a tendril of smoke drift from a window of one of the apartments. Fire? He wasn't taking any chances. He pulled out his phone and dialed 911 as he walked toward the building.

"What's going on?" Emma asked, standing right behind him just as the dispatcher answered the call.

"I want to report a fire at..." great, he didn't know the address. He spun around, kneeling down in front of Emma. "What's your address?"

"615 Grace Road, apartment 204," she said, smiling with pride. Then she frowned. "Did you say fire?"

Nik ignored her, repeating the address to the dispatcher and was told that it was already reported. Trucks were on their way.

And just as he finished the call, he saw people exiting the apartment, running out the front as well as the back. All were carrying what they could, leaving as quickly as possible.

He didn't see Claire.

"Which door do you guys go through when you come out of the building?" he asked Emma, holding her shoulder, just in case she panicked and ran toward the apartment.

"That one," Emma said, pointing as more people poured out of the doors, all of them calling out to each other, some crying. "But what's happening? Why are all those people coming out? Where's my mom? I have to get Mooch." Her voice rose with alarm and when she tried to run past him, he caught her and held her back.

She kicked and fought him, leaning toward the building, crying, picking up on the panicked cries of the people now running from the building. Mooch was barking and then a man stopped, releasing him. But thankfully he ran through the fence toward them.

At that moment, Nik didn't care if the dog took up residence in the flower bed. He was okay. They needed to get Claire.

"Mommy. I want my mommy," Emma cried.

He heard the sound of sirens.

"You have to wait, sweetie," he said, holding Emma against him. "The firemen are coming. They'll get your mommy out of the building."

"But she's not coming. Everyone else is out," Emma wailed again.

No one was coming out of the building anymore and Nik didn't know what to do. He had to watch Emma but he was getting worried about Claire.

Then, just as the firemen pulled up to the front of the building, the back door of the apartment opened again, and Claire stood, clinging to the door jamb, her face pale.

"There she is," Nik said to Emma. He set her down, his hands still on her shoulders, his voice hard and firm. "I'll go get her. You stay here. It's too dangerous for you."

He knew he was frightening her, but he had to make himself clear.

Emma sniffed and nodded, tears streaking down her face.

Nik paused another second to make sure she understood then he turned, ducked through the opening in the fence and ran toward Claire. She hobbled down the sidewalk, her face screwed up in pain.

He made it to her side and caught her as she faltered.

"We need to get out of here," he said, slipping his arm around her waist.

"Where's Emma? I thought I saw her here? I need to make sure Emma is okay," she cried with alarm, looking frantically around.

"She's okay. She's in my yard. So is the dog. We gotta go."

Nik glanced up at the building, but no flames were coming out of the windows yet.

Claire hobbled along, clinging to him, wincing each time she put weight on her foot.

"I need to get Emma and Mooch," she said puffing with exertion, glancing back over her shoulder as firemen came running around the building to the door she just exited. "Can you bring me to my car?"

"You can't drive. We'll take my truck. You need to see a doctor."

"I'm fine," she muttered yet clung to him as he helped her through the gap in the fence.

"Mommy, there you are," Emma cried, running toward them.

"Easy girl," Nik warned as Emma reached for Claire. "Your mother is hurt."

"Just twisted my ankle," she said. He could tell she wanted to pull away from him, but they had no idea how bad it was, so he kept his hold on her.

Despite the drama unfolding around them, he thought, for a moment, how nice it felt to hold a woman in his arms.

"Let's go to my truck. I think we should get out of here," Nik said, shaking off his reaction. He was just helping her, not hugging her, for pity's sake.

"But what about my stuff?" Emma cried. "I need to get my dolls and toys."

Nik caught her by one arm as she rushed past him. "Sorry, Emma. You need to stay out of the building. There's a fire inside."

Emma cried again, Mooch joined in with a howl and Nik felt out of his depth.

"Emma, stop it honey. Mr. Austen is right. We

can't go to the apartment." Claire tried to straighten but winced again and almost fell against him.

"But it's not burning," she exclaimed, swiping at her face.

"We don't know what's happening inside so we have to leave," Claire said, her voice strained. "Now please, let's go to Mr. Austen's truck."

"We need to take your mom to the hospital," he told Emma, hoping the little girl would listen. "That's the most important thing right now."

"But we can come back later, right?"

"We'll see," Claire said, leaning more on Nik. Just for a moment.

Nik led her to his truck, parked beside the house, and helped her in. Thankfully Emma followed and Mooch was right behind her.

A minute later they were driving away from the building and as Nik glanced in his rear-view mirror, part of him hoped the fire would extend to the house and burn it down. Save him the trouble of having to tear it down.

"You can just drop me off at the hospital," Claire said as he followed the directions she'd given him. "I'll get someone to come and pick me up."

Well, there was no way he was just dropping her off. Besides, she needed a place for her dog.

"Just tell me how to get there," he said, ignoring her comments. As he drove, he glanced over at her, not sure he liked how pale she was.

"It's just your ankle?" he asked.

"Yeah."

"You look like you're in a lot of pain."

"I've felt better," she said, "but I'll be okay."

Nik said nothing to that, just turned off the main road when she told him to. Emma sat in the back, sniffling a bit. In spite of her pain, Claire looked back at her, assuring her that everything would be okay.

A few minutes later they were at the hospital.

"Mooch has to stay in the truck," he said, warning Emma.

She patted her dog, looking concerned.

"He'll be okay," he assured her. "But wait until I open the door to let you out." He didn't want that out-of-control dog taking off on him. He got her out and kept Mooch in the cab of the truck with a stern 'no'. The dog whined but lay on the floor, his head on his paws, looking rather dejected.

As he closed the door, Claire was already struggling to get out.

"Here, let me help you," he said.

She waved him off but clung to the door, fighting to keep her balance. Stifling a sigh, he ignored her and tucked his arm around her to support her.

"I can manage," she said through clenched teeth.

Nik ignored her, as he shoved the door of the truck closed. He kept his steps slow and deliberate as he walked alongside her, not surprised when she leaned heavily on him. What did surprise him was the protective feeling that came over him as he helped her into the hospital.

And the appeal she created in him.

He shook that off as he brought her to the front desk. She was checked in and he helped her back to the deserted waiting room. But before she could even sit down, a nurse called Claire's name.

Once again, Claire waved off his assistance as she struggled to her feet. Once again, he ignored her, slipped his arm around her waist and he and Emma escorted her to an empty bed. As he settled her in, that protective feeing continued.

"Can I stay with you, Mommy?" Emma asked, her voice wobbling with emotion, clinging to Claire's hand.

"Yes you can, sweetheart," Claire said, stroking her daughter's shoulder.

"I'll just wait outside," Nik said, feeling rather out of place.

Claire looked up and gave him a wan smile. "Thanks for your help."

"Of course," he said releasing a light laugh. "What are neighbors for?"

Her face shifted and he caught a glimpse of sorrow. "Might not be neighbors anymore," she said.

She sounded exhausted and Nik didn't blame her. She had no idea if she had a place to stay or if any of her things would be salvageable. Everything for her was up in the air.

Then the nurse came with her clipboard, all capable and efficient. She glanced at Claire then Nik, a puzzled expression on her face.

"So, what brings you here, Claire?" she asked, sending another look Nik's way. Clearly this nurse knew Claire.

"I sprained my ankle trying to get out of my apartment."

"I think our 'partment is burning up," Emma put in, sniffing. "The firemen were there and everything and now my mommy is hurt."

"We heard about the fire, but the firemen said everyone got out okay."

"Except my mommy and now we don't have a place to stay," Emma continued, her voice trembling. "And I think my teddy bear is burnt up and all my toys."

"We don't know that for sure," Claire put in, patting Emma's shoulder. "The firemen came real quick. They probably put the fire out before it got to our place."

"Well, let's have a look at that ankle for now." The nurse glanced up at Nik. "I'm guessing you're the one who got Claire out?"

He waved off her question. "She was coming out and I helped her get here." He grew uncomfortable with the nurse's questioning glances. As if she were puzzling out how he and Claire were connected.

"A real hero," she said with a barely concealed grin, looking back at Claire.

"Don't start, Sarah," Claire said.

They did know each other.

"I'll just be outside," Nik said, taking a step away from the bed, and the knowing look the nurse named Sara gave Claire.

But as he left he heard Sarah say, "Pretty nice-looking guy, Claire."

"Be professional, please" Claire said, her voice prim and proper.

Nik hurried out of there.

Twenty minutes later, Claire hobbled out of the Emergency Room on crutches, her leg wrapped in a tensor bandage. Emma was carrying her other shoe, looking concerned.

"What did the doctor say?" Nik asked.

"A sprain. The usual. Rest and elevate it."

"And ice it I'm sure."

She blew out a sigh. "Well, thanks again for all your help."

"I can bring you home. You'll still need a ride." But no sooner had he spoken the words than he realized how silly that was.

She didn't have a home.

"Sorry. Not thinking," he said. "What are you going to do?"

A frown of worry creased her forehead. "I'll need to find another place to stay, I guess."

"We can stay in the house," Emma suggested, her face bright. "It's going to be our house now that you have the money, right?"

"You have the money?" Nik asked, surprised. Devon had assured him Claire had no chance of pulling it off. In fact, Devon was so sure that Nik had already been working on an application for re-zoning the property to a multi-family dwelling.

"I have a post-dated check from my cousin waiting to clear the bank." Claire gave him a weary smile. "Once that goes through, I'll have the full down payment."

Nik returned her smile but knew first chance he had he would call Devon to find out what was going on.

Claire still needed a place to stay, however.

"So where should I bring you?" he asked.

"To the house, of course, you silly," Emma said, sounding puzzled. "Our house."

Claire shook her head. "No, honey. It's not our house yet. I'll call Gramma. We can go there."

"But Gramma and Grandpa's house is full. She told me we couldn't stay there when I asked if I could," Emma said.

Claire bit her lip as she remembered this piece of news, then eased herself down into the chair behind her, looking drawn and tired. "Maybe we can go back into the apartment."

"We should find out," Emma said, clasping her hands in front of her as if she were praying. "Maybe everything will be okay."

Nik doubted that. Though he hadn't seen actual flames, he'd seen smoke. Even if the fireman put the fire out, the building would have to be repaired and inspected before anyone could move back.

"Can you take us there so we can see for sure?" Emma asked, turning to Nik.

Nik wanted to say no, but he guessed Emma wouldn't be satisfied until she knew for sure.

"Okay," Nik said, though he could guess what the outcome would be.

As they drove back to the apartment, Claire tried to make a few more calls, but it sounded to Nik like she wasn't having any luck finding a place to stay. No places to rent and because of a big volleyball tournament in town that weekend, no motel or hotel to stay at.

Emma's suggestion teased his mind. He could let them stay in the house. He was living in his trailer now and had figured on doing so until the new building was up. The house and its dark memories held no appeal to him.

But he wasn't sure he wanted Claire and her daughter staying so close, slowing down his plans.

The firemen were still at the apartments when they arrived, and Claire stumbled out of the truck before he could help her. Nik let Emma out but made Mooch stay. He wasn't sure where he would bring them next. He caught up to Claire as she was talking to one of the firemen.

"Sorry, lady. But no. We can't let anyone in until we've done a structural assessment," the fireman said, his face streaked with sweat and soot.

"I understand," Claire said, but as the fireman left to take care of another job, Nik caught the glint of tears in her eyes. She dropped her head for a moment.

She turned to him and he gave a careful smile, knowing he was doing the right thing, just not so sure it was the smart thing.

"You may as well stay in the house," he said, the finality of the words making him cringe.

"Really? Yay." Emma tossed herself at him and he caught her as she hugged his waist. "You're the best, Mr. Nik."

He looked past her, rather uncomfortable, glancing at Claire.

Her smile fell into his heart. And the little girl clinging to him filled a space in his empty soul.

With a quick pat on Emma's head, he pulled himself away from her.

"Good thing the house is furnished," he said. "Let's see about getting you two settled."

"We'll need toothbrushes and undies," Emma

said, bouncing from one foot to the other, pleased with how things had gone.

"We can get those ourselves," Claire said, reprimanding her daughter. "Besides, I need to stop at the cafe and talk to Tess. See about work today."

"Are you sure you're okay to work?" Nik asked.

Claire shrugged. "We'll see."

"And I'll take you wherever you need to go," he added.

Claire looked prepared to object again, but she seemed to give in.

They all went back to the truck, Nik supporting Claire again, surprised by the solicitous feeling she brought about.

He quashed it. He was just helping. Once they found a place, they would be out of the house and he could carry on with his plans.

He had to make sure he kept himself removed from them so when it was time to leave, he could move away with a clear head and no looking back.

CHAPTER 4

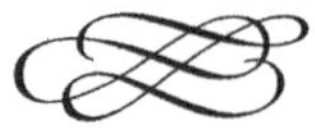

"May I sleep in my room?" Emma asked as they stepped into the house.

"I suppose you can," Claire said. "We'll have to look for some bedding."

But Emma was already thundering up the wide, wooden stairs, heading to "her room", which was Claire's old bedroom.

"Do you want this in here, or upstairs?"

Nik appeared beside her holding a box of clothes they had salvaged from the apartment once the firemen said it was okay to go inside.

They were warned repeatedly that they could only take personal items for the time being. No furniture, no large items. Only clothes and toiletries. Claire had grabbed her laptop and some bedding.

It had been exhausting going through an apartment that reeked of smoke, reliving that panicky moment when she wondered if she would get out okay, worried about Emma. On top of all that, she had to make quick decisions, under pressure with Nik watching and Emma making outrageous choices. It had been humiliating having Nik help her. And rather personal. Looking at her stuff through his eyes made her realize how shabby and worn her furniture was. How few items of value she owned.

Yet she desperately hoped they could return to the apartment and take everything else. Thankfully the fire hadn't reached her apartment, though it smelled of smoke. The thought of having to deal with the insurance company gave her the heebie jeebies.

Coffee Creek was taken care of for now, so that was good. When they stopped at the café, Tess had given her a huge hug and told her not to worry. She would call up Cory if she needed help.

Claire glanced at the box Nik held.

"Just put that in the room at the end of the hallway," she said, trying not to sound as tired as she felt. Her head throbbed as much as her ankle did as she followed Nik down the hall to her parents' old bedroom.

When Emma had blithely suggested they move into the house, Claire had brushed it off as the imaginings of an optimistic child. Nik was renting the place, after all.

But phone call after phone call had yielded no results. The vacancy rate for apartments in town was at a record low.

Tess lived in a tiny apartment that, Claire knew, was packed with wedding stuff. And Cory lived with her mother.

No room anywhere, except this house, which would probably be hers come Monday.

Despite all the plans she had made, the dreams she had spun around returning to this house; it still felt odd to step inside the bedroom that used to be first her parents', and then Mrs. Blatchford's.

Mrs. Blatchford had left the heavy ornate bed behind as well as the dresser with its old-fashioned oval mirror and tiny drawers for jewelry and knickknacks. Another, equally dark and heavy armoire was pushed into one corner of the room.

Dust covered every surface and Claire felt a pang of dismay at the lack of care and, at the same time, the work that lay ahead of her when she took over this house.

If she took over the house.

Think positive thoughts, she reminded herself. *This will all come together.*

"So, this is the master bedroom." Nik's voice held a note of bitterness.

“It looks like you haven’t slept here,” Claire said, as she glanced around.

"Not a chance," he returned. “I crashed on the couch and as soon as I got my trailer, I was out of here."

This puzzled her, but she wasn't about to get into his sleeping arrangements.

He set the box on the bed. "So, who of your family slept here?"

"My parents," she said, looking around the spacious room, other memories intruding. She hadn't been in this room since they’d moved out.

"You're smiling. What are you remembering?" he asked, the hard note still edging his voice.

Claire shifted her weight, her mind sifting backward to a happier time for her family. "Just odds and ends. Silly things, really," she said. She doubted he would be interested.

"Tell me."

"My mom always made my dad a cup of coffee

in the morning. She would bring it to him and they would sit in bed and drink it, planning out the day. On our birthdays, Tess and I could sit on the bed with our parents and unwrap our presents and drink coffee with them." She released a light laugh. "Just a little tradition we had."

"That sounds nice."

"What about you? What memories do you have?"

His expression grew hard, his eyes narrow, and he shrugged off her question. "I was never allowed in this room."

"Oh, trust me, neither were we. Just on our birthdays," she said.

"So, it was only you and your sister in this house?"

"Yeah. My mom didn't want more children. She always joked that we were too expensive. That my sister and I were noisy enough. But we had a lot of fun here." She smiled again.

She shifted her weight and a throb of pain revisited, reminding her of the present.

"I should get Emma in bed," she said. "She'll be one tired little girl."

Nik thankfully, didn't offer to help. Being around him had been more difficult than she'd liked. He was appealing and helpful and she was tired and lonely. Too easily she resurrected the strength of his arm supporting her, holding her up as he helped her walk to the hospital.

"Okay. Well, I hope you manage." Then he pulled out his cell-phone. "Why don't you give me your number and I'll plug it in and you can do the same? Just in case."

She hesitated a moment, feeling that swapping cell-phone numbers would be one more intrusion into her life.

She was being foolish. He was right there on the yard. If something happened to her, he would be the best person to call.

She tapped his number into her phone then slipped it in her back pocket, glancing up at him.

"Thanks again. For all your help. And for letting us stay in the house."

Nik paused and for a moment Claire thought he would say something. But he just walked out of the room.

His footsteps echoed in the empty house and as the door closed, Claire felt like she could breathe again. He created a confused rush of emotions she wasn't equipped to deal with.

She sighed, fighting down a wave of guilt over staying in the house he was renting, feeling like she and Emma were messing up his plans.

Well, they were *her* plans first. She and Mrs. Blatchford had an agreement long before Nik showed up on the scene and soon, this house would be hers.

As long as Tom's check went through.

The distressing thought wiggled to the forefront of her thoughts but she pushed it aside. Tom was her cousin. He wouldn't short-shrift her.

* * *

"I THOUGHT you told me she wouldn't get the money together," Nik said, switching his phone from one ear to the other as he toed off his shoes.

He had called Devon as soon as he could to find out what was going on.

"I didn't think she would, either," Devon said, sounding defensive. "But it's not a done deal, don't forget. That check has to clear the bank first."

Nik shoved his hand through his hair. He sat in the chair at one end of the trailer, wondering how he had ended up in this place. He hated it when plans changed or didn't go as expected.

A woman he was unwillingly attracted to was staying in the house that, unfortunately, didn't burn down. Her daughter, who created a welter of emotions as well, slept upstairs. And he still wasn't sure if the place would be his or not.

"I guarantee you your deal will go through," Devon said. "We only need a few more days and we can get to work. I'm not worried about the sale. I know the guy Claire sold the car too. Tom's a loser in every sense of the word. I'm positive he doesn't have the money to cover that check and only wrote it to keep Claire off his back."

Nik looked around his trailer, stifling a sigh of irritation. His gut told him he should walk away and be done with this hassle. Things were getting complicated and if there was one thing Nik had learned to avoid, it was convoluted business deals. They never went well. Especially when his emotions were involved — as they were now.

"Trust me, Nik, this will all come together," Devon continued. "Besides, you knew I had another offer on the house when you put yours in. You knew you'd be waiting. Nothing's changed."

Despite his frustration Nik had to concede that point.

"Didn't you tell me you were in town to do some visiting?" Devon added. "It's not like you're wasting your time there."

Nik leaned back in his chair, his mind ticking

back to the visit with his mother and Cory. He thought seeing his mother would answer questions, fill an emptiness that had grown deeper with every passing year. Instead, he felt like things had been left hanging and he wasn't sure of his next step.

That was why he had left town for a couple of days. Not only to pick up his trailer so he could live in it while he was working here, but to give him some time to think and re-orient himself.

Yet he kept circling back to the fact that Joyce was his mother… and, even better, he had a sister he hadn't known about. The family he had always yearned for.

"It'll be fine," Devon assured him again. "That house will be yours come Monday. Guaranteed."

"I hope you're right."

Nik said goodbye, then set the phone on the desk beside his chair. He leaned back, stretching, thinking, planning. He needed to get things ready to present to the town council. Needed to do some background work on town by-laws and current zoning regulations. Needed to find people to tear the house down and take the material away.

A light flickered on from a room upstairs in

the house, catching his attention. Nik suspected that's where Emma was sleeping.

As he watched a figure slowly walked past the window. Claire, he realized. She disappeared, then came back to the window, looking out. Directly at him.

He wanted to pull back, but it was too late. She knew he was watching her. Then, to his surprise, she gave him a little wave and pulled the blinds closed.

The light flicked out and he guessed Claire was on her way down the stairs. He hoped she wouldn't hurt herself. He shrugged his concern aside. He had other things to worry about. Cory wanted him to come for another visit tomorrow and he had agreed. Visiting Joyce would still be difficult, but he hoped it would be easier than the first time.

When it was time to go he wanted to leave with a clear conscience and a decent connection to the only family he had left.

CHAPTER 5

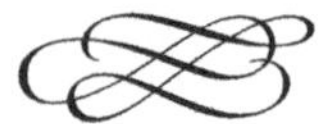

It had been a long night.

Claire picked up her phone, glanced at the screen and groaned when all she saw was black. Her phone was dead

The sun was just coming up, so it had to be 6:00 at the earliest. Her ankle throbbed, and she'd tossed and turned for the past hour. Between waves of pain she had alternately worried and prayed, thinking about her apartment and her stuff and how she would get through the next few weeks with what she had.

She hauled herself out of bed, re-wrapped the tensor, slipped on a pair of loose yoga pants and t-shirt, fumbled for her crutches and hobbled to the bathroom just across the hall.

This time of year the sun was just flirting with the horizon, sending out a faint glow over the mountains, promising day would come soon.

But inside, the house was still dark. She heard the rumble of the furnace turning on and despite the pain burning in her ankle; she smiled. As a little girl she used to lay tucked up in her bed upstairs, blankets wrapped around her, waiting for that very sound. It was often the signal that her mother was up and had turned up the thermostat. Claire would come downstairs and sit on one of the registers in the kitchen, heat billowing her nightgown, drinking a huge cup of milk-tea, watching her mother pack lunches for the day and put breakfast on the table. Her father would come down the hall, smiling. He'd give her mom a hug and they would share a kiss. They were so happy then.

Claire doused the memories and turned on the light in the bathroom. She winced as she rummaged through the cosmetic bag she had hastily filled up yesterday, looking for pain killers. Nothing.

When they went to her apartment yesterday, Claire was keenly aware of the fireman who had accompanied her, hovering in the doorway and the urgency he projected. So she had grabbed the bare minimum. And, in her defense, her ankle didn't hurt much at that time, thanks to the hospital's potent painkillers. But those had worn off, and the agony had returned.

She leaned back against the door, fighting off the painful throbbing as blood pooled in her ankle. She needed to get to the drugstore. But she had promised Emma she could sleep in. Emma was a grump first thing in the morning so riding out the pain was probably easier than listening to her daughter's grumbling.

Coffee was her only option.

But as she scrambled down the hall, another reality snuffed out that tendril of hope.

She hadn't thought to grab groceries out of the kitchen cupboards in the apartment.

And she had just bought a container of coffee the other day. Her mouth watered thinking about it. So close and yet so far.

Claire paused in the kitchen a moment, looking around the open space and allowed herself a moment of gratitude. Soon this would be her and her daughter's place. Soon she could give Emma the proper home she'd always wanted.

Please, Lord, she prayed, *let it all work out.*

She heard the jingle of dog-tags. Mooch had heard her rummaging about and was coming down the stairs. He walked up beside her, whining. He needed to go out.

Claire patted him absently on the head then stumped to the back of the house and opened one of the double French doors.

Mooch barreled past her and, to her dismay, headed directly for the flower beds.

"Mooch, stop. Come back here." He stopped, looked back at her, took a few steps toward the flower beds just as she called him again. He didn't come to her, but stood, staring at the corner of the yard whining. Seriously, they had to find whatever it was he had buried in there before he destroyed it completely.

"Do you think he'll listen?"

The deep voice beside her made her jump which sent pain shooting through her ankle. She faltered and might have fallen but, once again, Nik held her up. Her first reaction was to push him away, but that would cause more problems, so she stayed where she was.

His hand was large, and warm. And as she glanced up at him, she saw his cheeks were flushed and his hair damp. He looked like he had been running.

"Sorry about that," she said, disappointed at how out of breath she sounded. She wavered a moment as she caught her balance and then, thankfully, he released his hold on her.

"That dog sure likes that flower bed," Nik said dropping his hands on his hips as he breathed in and out, sounding winded.

"I'm sure he's got something buried there that he wants to dig up." She turned back to the dog. "Mooch. Come here." Thankfully, this time he trotted back, head down, disappointment flowing off him in waves. He dropped beside her with a whine but stayed put.

"So, he's used to coming and going as he pleases if he's burying stuff in this yard," Nik said.

"Mrs. Blatchford didn't mind and encouraged Emma and Mooch to play in the yard." Claire leaned on her crutches lifting her foot to ease the pain. "So, he's pretty lackadaisical about territory, as I'm sure you've noticed."

His chuckle surprised her. He always looked so serious. Then he looked over at her apartment. "I don't suppose you have any idea when they'll let you back in?"

"I'm hoping to call somebody today to find out. Although, quite frankly, I wouldn't be surprised if they condemn it. It's old and worn down, people shouldn't even be living in it."

"But you did," Nik said.

"It was the only place available," Claire said. She wasn't adding that it was also the only place she could afford. That might make her sound like a loser.

"There don't seem to be a lot of rental properties here in Sweet Creek," Nik said.

"That's why I am squatting here," Claire said. "And thanks again for letting me stay. I promise to get out of your hair as soon as possible."

She looked up at the sky, which grew lighter as the sun came up. "Do you mind telling me what time it is?"

"About 6:30. Why?"

"My phone died and I'm just trying to figure out when's a reasonable time to wake Emma up so I can go buy coffee. There's none in the house."

"Yeah, I didn't stock the kitchen up when I moved in. I hadn't figured on staying in it long."

His comment hung between them, heavy with its import. He hadn't figured on staying in it because he had planned on living in his trailer. While he tore down the house.

"I've got some coffee brewing in the trailer," Nik said, breaking the momentary silence. "If you are as addicted as me, you might not want to wait until Emma wakes up."

Claire hesitated, but the need for caffeine

overrode her resistance to spending more time with Nik. She was too touchy about him. After all, he had practically carried her out of the apartment. A few boundaries between them had already come down.

In that moment of hesitation, he seemed to get his answer.

"Black or cream and sugar?" he asked.

"Just black please," she said.

"I'll be right back," he said then turned and strode to the trailer.

Claire's foot throbbed and she eased herself onto the step, stretching her leg out in front of her. Thankfully, it was nice and warm so sitting outside was pleasant.

As promised, Nik returned with not one, but two steaming mugs.

"I haven't had mine yet either," he explained as he handed one to her. Then, to her surprise, he sat on the step beside her.

Claire wasn't sure what to make of this, but it was enjoyable to drink coffee in the morning with an adult.

"So how did your visit with your mother go?" she asked, taking a sip of the hot brew. She cradled her hands around the mug, drawing from its warmth.

Nik leaned his elbows on his knees, holding his mug as he stared at the trailer. "It was… okay."

"I'm sure it was hard," Claire said. "After all, you barely knew her."

"I was about four years old when I got adopted," Nik said. He took a sip of his coffee. "Old enough to have some fairly strong memories of her."

Claire knew she was venturing into shaky territory by asking questions; getting too involved.

But her life had turned upside down and the only person who had been there for her was this stranger.

So she stifled her second thoughts.

"What do you remember about her?" she asked.

Nik sighed then took another sip of his coffee looking away, and for a moment Claire wondered if she had gone too far.

But he blinked then gave her a careful smile. "I remember her holding me on her lap and reading a book. I can't recall which book, only that it had a picture of a rabbit with a bright red hat. I don't remember my father. Apparently, he died when I was a baby. He was a carpenter, too." He pulled in a long, slow breath and eased it out.

"Too? Is that what you do? Build houses?"

"Sometimes. I'll rehab them if they're good enough, tear them down and do an infill if they aren't. Then I sell them and move on."

"You've never lived in the places you work on?"

He shook his head. "No. Once I'm done, I'm gone. I don't like getting too attached. I like my freedom."

"So you've never owned a home?"

Once again, he was quiet, drinking his coffee.

"I had a house. Once."

"What happened?"

He took another sip as silence fell between them and he looked away from her.

The door behind them creaked open, breaking the now-awkward quiet.

"Hi, Mom. Can I get up?"

Emma stood on the porch in her nightgown, one foot layered over the other, hugging herself. Her hair was a tousle of curls and her cheek still held the faint imprint of her hand.

"Of course you can," Claire said, setting her mug on the step below her and holding out her arms for Emma.

"Hello, Mr. Nik," Emma said, yawning as she curled up on Claire's lap.

Claire smoothed Emma's unruly hair back

from her face, then laid her cheek on Emma's head, inhaling the sleepy, little girl smell of her. "How did you sleep, punkin?"

"Great. This house smells so good. And I don't have to listen to the people fighting in the 'partment beside us." She yawned — a jaw-cracking yawn — and cuddled closer to Claire. "Can we go back and get more of my stuff? I don't have all my dolls or stuffies."

"I don't know, honey," Claire said, feeling a pang herself for the things she'd left behind.

"Do you think you could go with me, Mr. Nik?" Emma asked.

Nik half-turned, glancing at the two of them. A curious expression flitted across his face. "I doubt we're allowed," he said.

"But no one is there now. We could just sneak in." Emma lifted her head, trying to look over the fence at the building. "If we're quiet no one will know we're there."

"I don't think it matters how quiet we are," Nik said. "It isn't safe."

"But I'm not very big. I won't fall through the floor. I can crawl real good. And I know how to be real quiet. Sneaky quiet."

To Claire's surprise, Nik sputtered then took a quick swig of his coffee as if to cover up his reaction to her daughter and her incessant finagling.

"Honey, there was a fire in the building. We don't know what it's like inside. We can't go back," Claire reiterated.

"But we went back for *some* of our stuff," Emma continued, her voice wavering. "Why can't we go again?"

"The firemen were there to make sure we didn't hurt ourselves and that we were safe. They're not there now."

Emma opened her mouth to protest but Claire gently placed a finger on her lips. "And I'm sorry you don't have all your toys, we're not talking about this anymore and there's no way we are even thinking about going to the apartment again." She had to be firm. If she wasn't, she was afraid Emma might sneak over, though she was fairly sure the doors were locked.

"Well, I'm hungry," Emma said, hugging her knees, resting her head on them.

"I am too, so we need to get some groceries. And a pill for my ankle." Claire picked up her coffee and drank it down.

"Well, I'd better get back to work," Nik said, pushing himself to his feet.

"What are you working on?" Emma asked.

"Some blueprints," he said, evasively. Not that it was any of their business, but Claire suspected his plans had everything to do with the house behind them.

"Those are like plans right?"

"That's right," Nik said.

"Maybe you can make some plans for my mommy. She said she wants to make a bigger deck on here. So she can sit on a chair and look over the yard. She used to live here, you know?" Emma prattled on, delightfully unaware of the shift in the atmosphere.

Claire was reminded how tenuous her hold on this house was and once again she sent up a quick prayer that the check would clear. God had larger things to deal with, but she had always been encouraged to lay her troubles at his feet. Well, this was a trouble out of her control.

"Here's my cup," she said, sparing Nik the trouble of finding an answer to her daughter's question. "As for you, Missy," she said to Emma, "you need to get dressed so we can go out."

Emma scrambled over Claire and in the process, tripped over Claire's ankle. Oblivious to her mother's sudden indrawn gasp of pain, she skipped across the deck and into the house.

"You okay?" Nik asked.

"Yeah. I'll be fine." She pulled in another breath through her clenched teeth, riding out the pain, her hands tight fists.

"I don't think you should drive yet," Nik said. "Why don't I take you?"

She shook her head. "I'll call my parents," she said, then made a face. Her phone was dead. She wasn't calling anyone.

"I'm right here. I'm not doing much else. Let me be a good neighbor."

He was being more than a good neighbor, she thought. She and her daughter were sleeping in the house he was paying rent on. He had taken her to the hospital and had helped bring her things from the apartment to the house. She owed him a lot more than she could ever repay and didn't want to be driven further into his debt.

However, she needed to be realistic. Driving would be painful and probably unsafe. She couldn't call anyone unless she borrowed his cell phone.

"Okay, but you have to let me pay you for the gas."

Nik shot her a look of disbelief. "Sure. In a town the size of Sweet Creek, that will probably come to about ninety-seven cents," he said.

She laughed. "Okay. I get it. But I don't feel right about all this."

"Someday you can pay it forward," he said. "So, let's leave it at that."

She slowly got to her feet, hoping he would let her stand on her own. But also, in some part of her lonely female brain, she hoped he would give her a gentle boost. She managed to stand on her own.

Too bad.

"I'll meet you out front," he said, poking his thumb over his shoulder to where his truck was parked. "Unless you need a hand?"

She shook her head. "I'll be okay. I just need to get my purse and make sure Emma's ready to go."

She turned to go back into the house, far too conscious of Nik's eyes on her.

* * *

WAS he being smart about the situation, Nik wondered, as he stepped into his trailer.

Spending time with a single, attractive woman who was hoping to buy the same house he was?

And what about her daughter?

Despite the discomfort she initially created, Emma made him laugh. She was spunky and fun and very much alive. This had surprised him. When he heard about the baby his girlfriend had swept from her life, he had been angry, hurt, frustrated. And for years afterward, seeing any child the same age as their baby would have been, brought up the pain of loss.

But somehow, being with Emma, those feelings eased.

Don't get attached. Be the first to leave.

Nik shook his head and made do with a quick wash-up and a change of clothes.

He could hardly turn his back on an injured woman and her young daughter. Sure, she had relatives and friends, but he was close, and available.

Nik grabbed his keys from the tray beside his bed, shoved his wallet in his pants and ran his fingers through his hair again, wishing he'd had time to have a shower.

He glanced around the inside of his newer living quarters, thankful for the space and that he was out of the house.

Though many years had passed since those dark days, staying here had resurrected those memories. Memories of fear and pain and hours spent alone. The uncertainty of what the day would bring when he got up in the morning.

Some days were good. And some — the days that Rick Baley came home drunk — not so good.

Thankfully, Nik was no longer that scared kid. He had dealt with those demons, and they would be exorcised once the house was pulled down and the reminder of that time eradicated.

His phone buzzed and he pulled it out of his pocket. Cory.

"Hey, how are you doing?" he asked, his heart giving a little lift. His sister, he thought, a half-sister, but still. The idea would never grow old.

"I'm good. But, about tonight…" she let the word trail away and Nik figured out what was next.

"Your mom wants to cancel?" He struggled to keep his annoyance from entering his voice.

"She doesn't want to. She's exhausted today. It's not something she can help." Cory sounded defensive.

Nik pulled in a slow breath, realizing the emotions swirling through him were a combination of frustration and, if he were honest, disappointment.

"That's too bad. It's just… this was the reason I came here."

"She really wants to see you," Cory said. "Her fibro is often brought on by stress and much as she's excited to see you, her emotions bring on stress, which triggers her fibro. It's a vicious cycle."

"Okay. What about tonight? You and me getting together?"

"I'd love to, but Matthew and I have an appointment with our wedding photographer. I'd try to get out of it, but we had a hard enough time getting him in the first place, he's so busy. I could call him—"

"Don't. It's my fault for jumping into your lives without giving you advance notice. Keep the appointment. What about Sunday?"

This elicited another sigh. "I'm so sorry. After seeing the photographer, we're getting together with Matthew's parents in Edmonton. It's a long drive so we're staying overnight. We won't be back until late Sunday night. But you could visit Mom on your own."

Nik paused, surprised at his unwillingness to do that.

"Or maybe it would be best if I'm there," Cory added quickly. "So, let's make it Monday night, and I'll tell Mom that it's happening no matter what."

Despite his frustration, Nik smiled at the firm note in Cory's voice. "Then I'll figure on that."

They said goodbye and as Nik shoved his phone in his pocket he struggled with the anger his memories of his mother could create. The sorrow. It was exhausting, and, over time, it had lost its sharp angles but it stayed, weighing him down.

Yet, these past few days weren't how he had envisioned his reunion with his mother.

One step at a time, he reminded himself. *Like you told Cory, you just jumped into their lives. And you'll be here a while.*

Unless Claire gets the house. Then what happens to your plans?

He wished he could just walk away. But this house had been a dark shadow over his life. He couldn't do anything about his foster parents, but he could do something about the house

He walked across the yard just as Emma bounded out of the door. Claire's oversized purse hung from her scrawny shoulder and she turned to hold the door open for her mother.

"Do you need a hand?" he asked as the door fell shut behind Claire.

She had changed as well and now wore a soft pink shirt with large white polka dots and white cropped pants with flats. Her hair flowed loose and a faint breeze lifted it off her shoulders. For a moment he was transfixed. She was gorgeous.

Then Nik saw Emma and reality tempered his admiration. Though he wasn't as uncomfortable around the little girl as he initially was, she was a reminder of why he had to keep his admiration to himself.

His plans couldn't include women, especially not women who came with kids. Too complicated and not fair to the child.

Emma grunted as she tried to shift the purse to her other shoulder and almost dropped it.

"Why don't you let me carry that?" Nik said.

"It's really heavy." Emma grimaced as she handed it over, barely able to keep it off the ground.

"No kidding," Nik said as he took it from her. He glanced at Claire, lifting it up and down as if guessing its weight. "What do you have in here?"

Claire held up a hand to stop him, shooting him a warning glance. "Don't start with the brick-in-the purse jokes."

"Well, if it's not a brick, then maybe a rock."

Emma giggled and, despite his caution Nik felt a curious lift of his heart.

"So where's the dog?" he asked.

"Mooch is inside. He'll be okay," Claire said,

giving him a careful smile which hindered his resolve. "We've had to leave him in the apartment from time to time. He's usually fine."

Nik wasn't too sure about that, but he wasn't arguing. What did he care if the dog tore things apart in the house?

"Okay, let's go then," Nik said.

Ignoring Claire's protests, he helped her into his truck, feeling that momentary spark of attraction as he held her arm and supported her; her hair brushing his face.

Emma settled in and soon they were on their way.

"Just turn left at the second set of lights," Claire said. "That's where I usually shop."

"Good to know. I'll need groceries, too," Nik said.

"Are you staying on the yard for very long?" Emma piped up from the back seat.

"Not sure," he said.

"Do you like living in your trailer? My mommy said she can't imagine why you would, but I think it looks cozy."

Nik shot Claire a glance, surprised to see her blushing. So, they were talking about him.

"I live in it often."

"That's kind of fun, but you can't have a play

center and swing and slide then. Like our house does."

Our house. Nik felt another flash of concern, and with it came second thoughts surrounding his purchase of the house.

He pushed them aside. He'd learned to hold plans loosely.

CHAPTER 6

"When will this place be ours?" Emma asked as Claire let herself into the house at the end of her long, arduous day.

Claire's heart tightened at her daughter's innocent question. Once again, she had to choke down her anger with her cousin and, if she were honest, with Devon. He knew how much this place meant to her.

This is strictly business, he had told her when she called him. Nothing personal.

His words still burned in her ears. She had wanted to believe he was telling the truth, but she also knew Devon wasn't happy with the selling price his mother had negotiated with Claire.

Now he didn't have to worry about it. Whatever Nik was paying him made him happier than with what Claire could afford.

"We'll talk about that after supper," Claire said, forcing a smile for her daughter.

"I like how this house smells," Emma said with a satisfied twirl around the kitchen. "And that chicken is making me hungry."

Claire had picked up a rotisserie chicken from the grocery store and taken a few leftovers from the coffee shop home with her for supper.

Today, she was exhausted. Physically, emotionally and spiritually.

"I want to go shopping for paint tomorrow," Emma said, dropping onto the window seat of the bay window. "And when can we get our furniture out of the apartment?"

Emma's innocent question added more layers of stress. "I talked to the fireman. He said we can get them Wednesday."

"I wish we could go tomorrow."

"Wednesday will be soon enough." Sooner than Claire wanted.

She had a lot of things to get in place before that. Once her daughter was in bed she needed to talk to Nik to see if he could give her a few days grace to find a new place to stay.

And where will you go? She thought. Now that

the weekend was over she might find a place in a motel. Which would mean finding somewhere to store her furniture come Wednesday.

Too much to think about. Too much to juggle.

"I see Mr. Nik is in his trailer," Emma said, hands pressed against the window. "Should I ask him if he wants to come for supper?"

"No. Absolutely not." Claire quickly replied, much harsher than she intended. "You have your baseball practice tonight, so we don't have time for company," she said, tempering her voice.

Emma made a pouty face. "I don't want to play baseball. I'm no good at it."

"That's why you have practice. Besides, you love your coach."

"Yeah. Miss Cory is awesome. So is Mr. Matthew. Did you know they are getting married?"

"Yes, I did.

"And even Chris' mom, Kelsey, is getting married. To someone named Ben."

"I know. I think that's nice for her." Claire set her crutches aside, thankful that her ankle was feeling better.

"Chris is lucky he gets a dad." Emma wrapped her arms around her legs. "I sure wish I had a dad."

Emma hadn't broached that topic for a few days so Claire, foolishly thought she had abandoned it.

Obviously not.

Claire pulled in a deep breath then walked over to her daughter, sitting beside her on the window seat. "Honey, we talked about this before," she said, pulling Emma close. "We have each other and that has to be enough for us. I love you more than anybody can, and we are a family."

Claire had often spoken these words to Emma but with her life falling apart around her, they sounded glib. And, worse, as if Claire was putting Emma off.

But Emma simply sighed, snuggling closer into her mother's arms. "I love you, mommy," she said.

Claire brushed a kiss over Emma's hair, then laid her cheek on her head. "And I love you, too. More than you can know."

"My teacher says I'm really smart, so you must love me lots."

"Tons," Claire said, easing out a thankful sigh.

Right now she didn't have the energy to deal with anything more.

* * *

"EMMA HASN'T BEEN super enthusiastic about practice," Claire warned Cory as she watched Emma trudge toward outfield, her head down.

Cory gave Claire a sympathetic smile. "I'm sure she's still dealing with the apartment fire."

"That and a few other things," Claire agreed.

"We'll watch out for her, won't we Matthew?"

Matthew, her fiancé, was chatting with Chris, Kelsey Swain's son, and gave Cory an absent nod.

"I doubt he heard that," Cory said with a grin and a shrug. "But we'll take extra care with her."

"Thanks." And once again, Claire was thankful for the community she was a part of. She made her way to the bleachers. Her ankle was still a bit sore, but she was thankful she didn't need her crutches.

Parents of Emma's teammates filled the first two rows and for a moment Claire sympathized with her daughter. Though she was thankful she didn't have to worry about Emma's father, there were times she missed having someone with her.

She gingerly made her way through the people to the top row of bleachers and sat down then rolled her eyes when she spotted her daughter. Emma sat on the grass, elbows planted on her knees, her head resting in her hands while the other children practiced.

Claire waved at her to stand up, but Emma ignored her.

All the way there, Emma had complained about coming and now she was making her protest known.

Claire's phone beeped and as she bent over her purse to see who it was, someone sat down beside her. She shot a sideways glance, smiling a greeting.

And then a chill slid down her spine.

Nik.

He must have come here to watch Cory coach.

"Hey there," she said, her smile freezing in place. Her phone buzzed again, and she pulled it out, thankful for a reason not to talk to him.

But the only thing on her screen was a notification for an update. She dropped it into her purse, fighting a very unwelcome desire to cry. Nik, sitting beside her, was the personification of all she had lost today. She thought, as soon as he had found out about getting the house, he would ask her to move out. But he hadn't contacted her at all.

She knew it was coming though.

She wrapped her arms around her purse, looking out over the field. Emma was now on her feet, looking ready to participate.

Be grateful for small miracles, Claire reminded herself.

Nik cleared his throat and, then, to her shock, he laid a gentle hand on her shoulder. "So, believe it or not, I'm sorry about the house," he said, his voice quiet.

Claire wasn't sure what to make of either the apology or the touch of his hand. The one made her feel good, but the other was a reminder of what she'd lost.

"I didn't meet the terms, so that's what happens." She chanced a quick glance his way, hoping to show him there were no hard feelings, but as soon as their eyes met and she saw the sympathy in his, her throat tightened.

Even worse, her eyes prickled.

She spun away, hunching her shoulders in a defensive posture. She wanted to make a lighthearted comment about her loser cousin but couldn't muster the self-control. And there was no way she was crying in front of him.

"I imagine you'll want me out of the house as soon as possible," she said. "So you can start… start working on it."

She heard Nik blow out a sigh and then he leaned forward, his elbows on his knees. "I know you'll need time to find another place to stay, so I want to make sure you have that."

"Thanks so much, I appreciate it." And to her dismay, her voice broke. And then, even more surprising, was the feel of Nik's hand, once again resting on her shoulder.

"Hey. I'm sorry. I know how much that house meant to you."

Claire closed her eyes. The touch of his hand, his nearness, prompted a yearning she hadn't felt in a long time. A yearning for someone who she could share life with. For someone she could turn to when things were difficult.

"Well, I'll just have to find another place, won't I?" she said with forced brightness. But she had gotten a bargain from Mrs. Blatchford. A bargain she could not easily replicate in Sweet Creek on her wage.

Her cell phone had the decency to ring, and she yanked it from her purse, thankful for the diversion. She didn't recognize the number but took the call anyway.

"Yeah, hi. This is Doug Sawatzki. I got the go-ahead from the Fire guys to let you into the apartment to get your stuff. I'm doing it on a rotating basis. I figured 'cause you're living next door it would be easiest to start with you. Only trouble is they only gave me ten days, so to save traffic I have to give all you guys a time limit and a hard date."

Claire scratched her forehead, thinking furiously. "So what's my hard date and time limit?"

"For you, I've got Tuesday afternoon booked."

"That's tomorrow. You told me Wednesday. How… why… I don't… I can't get all my stuff out. I don't have a place—"

"Sorry. Gotta be firm. Fire chief was pretty clear on the time-line. And I started with you 'cause, like I said, you're right next door."

"I'll need to arrange for a storage facility. I can't do that tomorrow."

"Well, that's why I called you now. So you've got tonight and the morning. But I gotta make a ton of other calls, so see you tomorrow." He hung up. Claire tossed her phone in her purse, sucking in a long, slow breath. Anger vied with fear as she stared at the ball diamond where her daughter was now enthusiastically chasing the baseballs Cory and Matthew were tossing the kids' way. At least she was happy.

"Everything okay?" Nik asked. "You look upset."

"I've got to get my stuff out of the apartment. And I've only got tomorrow afternoon to do it."

The words were out before she could stop them. She would not look at him. She had felt that same deep need for someone to share her problems with and he'd asked, so she'd turned to him.

His dark brown eyes held hers, sympathy still embedded in their depths.

"So what are you going to do?"

"I don't know." She didn't want to deal with any more problems, but she couldn't avoid this. "I guess I'll start with finding a storage place." A wave of exhaustion washed over her. No time. Too many things to deal with. "Then I need to find a place to live."

She shoved her hands through her hair, pushing it away from her face as she blew out another sigh.

"So you'll need a few more days in the house then and some help with moving your things."

He said it as if it were a given.

She hated that she was so deep in his debt. "A few more days should give me enough time to find another place," she said. "And as for moving the stuff out, I'm sure I can find someone to help."

"Well, I'm not doing much else. I can pitch in, too. Besides, I still owe you for supper the other night."

"Seriously? It was just pizza."

"Yeah, but it was nice to not eat by myself."

The faint note of melancholy in his voice caught her attention. "Well, it was nice to have help. Given I could hardly walk."

"So, it worked out for both of us."

They shared another look that probably went longer than it should have, creating a sense of longing.

"Besides, I'm not so hard-hearted that I would kick a single mom and her daughter out onto the streets," he said, giving her a crooked grin. "That wouldn't be good for business."

Despite everything she'd dealt with that day, in spite of the hovering headache, she felt a gentle warmth at his smile and at his comment. "So you're just worried about your reputation?" she teased.

His expression grew serious. "I know what it's like to be at the end of your rope. With no one to help you keep you hanging on."

She frowned at that, thinking of his comments about the house and what happened to him there. She had an urge to know more. To find out what made him want to destroy it.

Do you? Really? Don't you have enough stuff going on in your own life?

The questions grounded her, and she turned

back to look at Emma. To remind herself of her priority; her daughter and what *she* needed.

Besides, once Nik was done here, he would be gone. She couldn't allow herself to get too deeply involved in his life.

Even still, as she thought of him living on the yard of the house, she hoped she would be able to keep her distance.

CHAPTER 7

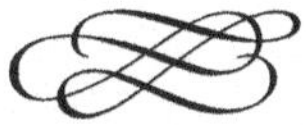

"I thought living in such a small space would have made you more of a minimalist," Tess complained as she set another box in the living room of the house.

"I read *The Joy of Cleaning up*. I only keep what gives me joy," Claire returned, pushing a box into the corner.

"Then you must be ecstatic," Tess groaned, arching her back to ease out a kink. "Isn't that book supposed to make you throw things away?"

"No. It's about caring for the things you have. And I care deeply about all this stuff."

"You need to read it again. I think you missed the basic concept."

Claire bopped her sister on the head with a pillow and they both laughed.

Nik chuckled at the give and take between the two. They'd been at it from the moment Tess and their mother came into Claire's apartment. He flashed back to a memory he had of them — years ago — walking down the street, holding hands and laughing. Two sisters who enjoyed each other's company. Then, as now, he was jealous of their easy relationship as siblings.

And once again he felt a surge of anger that his mother had taken that away from him.

"So where do you want this?" he asked, carrying a box into the room.

"Can you set it on the kitchen counter?" Claire asked. "There's spices and utensils in that box I might need."

"Can do." He carried it back through the arched entryway into the kitchen. Against Claire's strong protests, Tess had unpacked one of the boxes and put the same decorative tablecloth on the table as Claire had in her apartment and put the same plant on it as well. She'd hung a few prints on the walls and set some of Claire's knickknacks on the empty shelves. Before her mother, who was also helping with the move, left she had hung curtains on the rods of the bay window and set pictures on it stating that they needed to make the place homey.

Much as Nik hated to admit it, they *had* made the house cozier and inviting.

"Hey, just wanted to say thanks for all your help."

Nik turned to see Tess, hands on her hips, smiling at him. She walked over to the table, straightened the cloth and looked around. "I know that Claire couldn't buy this house, but I want to say, from my family, that we're thankful you're letting her and Emma stay here a while."

He wanted to ask her to define "a while". Her mother had said close to the same thing to him when she left earlier.

He said nothing, but he would have to discuss this with Claire once everyone was gone. If it wasn't for the fact that the equipment he'd lined up wouldn't arrive for a couple of weeks, he'd be tearing the house down right now. But he also needed to know Claire would have a place to stay before that happened.

"I'm glad to help," Nik said.

Tess lingered a moment, and Nik sensed she wanted to say something more. So he waited.

"I was chatting with Emma just a few moments ago," Tess said. She looked directly at him now, as if challenging him. "You may as well know she's been dropping heavy hints about what kind of father you would make. I hope you haven't encouraged her."

Anger was his first reaction. How could she think that when he had done nothing, said nothing?

But behind that came a lingering admiration for a sister who was only looking out for her sister and her niece.

"I have said nothing to her," was all he could come up with.

Tess didn't seem convinced.

"Look, I've got my own plans and they don't involve Emma or Claire. As soon as I can get this house torn down and my new building up, I'm out of here."

He said the words with more conviction than he felt. Sitting beside Claire at the baseball practice, watching his sister interact with the kids and with Emma had felt, for lack of a better word, *right*. He felt as if he were slowly being drawn into a place of belonging.

At the practice Cory had waved to him a couple of times and so had Emma. Allen Andrews had stopped by to ask him a few questions and one of the clerks from the grocery store he went to had also said hello.

"I'm sure you also understand how important this house is to Claire," Tess said.

Nik felt like he was being pushed into a corner, so he simply said nothing.

"I just want to give you permission not to feel too guilty about buying it," Tess said. "In spite of her tough as nails attitude, she's a sentimental softy. I've seen her cry over coffee commercials. And she has an idealized view of this house." Tess looked away from him, fiddling with a flap on the box she had set on the table. "Look, I've probably said too much. But I wanted to let you know we're all okay with this. You owning the house."

Nik wasn't sure what was expected of him, so he went with another vague smile.

"But there's something else I need to mention to you. As a protective auntie, I want to warn you that Emma is a romantic as well. So... just... please... be careful with her too."

Nik wanted to reassure her he would be.

But as the words were ready to come out, he hesitated. He was growing fond of Emma. She was a sweet, spunky girl, and she made him laugh. Something that he hadn't experienced for a very long time.

However, he understood what Tess was intimating.

"I absolutely will be," he assured her, holding her gaze. He was about to leave, but something she said about Claire's version of the house stuck with him. "You grew up in this house, too? How do you feel about it?"

Tess looked around the kitchen then shrugged. "I'm not as sentimental as Claire is, but then the boundaries of my life have fallen into pleasant places lately. I don't feel like I need to return to some special place in my life to find peace because I'm happy right now." She returned his look. "A lot of stuff in my past has been resolved, or I'm at least working through it. Claire, however, still struggles with issues from the past and from her ex." She stopped there.

"Her ex?" Nik asked. Claire had alluded to her ex-husband but only in the vaguest terms. "What issues is she struggling with?"

Tess sliced her hand in the air between them. "I don't want to say too much about that. Why do you want to know?"

He held her penetrating gaze then said, "Just curious." He knew it was a brush off and he also knew Tess didn't believe him.

"Just be careful with them," she said, giving him a cautious smile.

"I will," he said.

But as she left, he wandered to the doorway, and watched Claire stack up the boxes containing what she had salvaged from her apartment. She was in profile to him and she looked at the stairs, a half-smile playing around her mouth.

He turned away and set the box he held onto the counter, his emotions battling with the happiness he saw on her face. How she felt about this house shouldn't matter.

But even as he ripped open the box to set its contents on the counter, Claire's happiness sifted around his own feelings. Tapped lightly at his plans, and he wasn't sure how to feel about that.

* * *

"THANKS FOR FIXING THAT FOR ME," Claire said, glancing over at Nik. He stepped down from the kitchen chair he had dragged into the middle of the room and dropped the screwdriver into a toolbox he had carried into the house.

"Gladly done," he said.

"Of course, the irony of you repairing something in a house you'll be tearing down isn't lost on me." Nik heard the forced lightness in her tone and wished it didn't bother him.

"Having a smoke detector go off at midnight for no reason affects me, too," he said with a shrug.

"Makes sense." Claire gave him a careful smile, as if sensing his pretext.

These little connections had become more frequent lately. From both of them. Covert glances and quick greetings as they passed each other in the yard held more weight than they had before. It was a connection he knew he shouldn't encourage but couldn't stop himself from making.

So, when she called him to ask him to fix the smoke detector, he'd been far too happy to oblige.

"I made coffee, did you want some?" she asked. "Emma baked some cookies she wanted to give to you but didn't have time to bring them over."

"Where is she now?"

"Sleeping. She had a busy day at school and went to a birthday party afterwards. She was beat."

He felt a tinge of regret. He would have liked to have seen Emma.

He mentally shook off his reaction, his head

fighting with his heart. He was becoming too attached to that young girl and, even worse, her mother.

Things were shifting between him and Claire and moving to a nebulous place where they could reach an emotional tipping point. He knew he should leave, but the thought of returning to his empty trailer held no appeal.

"Sure. That sounds good." He looked for a place to sit by the table, but the chairs all held clothes and assorted items.

"Sorry about the mess. Emma's been digging around for some of her toys. We can go sit in the living room if that's okay."

"Fine by me." He preferred the living room anyway. Less drama had happened there than in this kitchen.

Claire picked up a tray and he let her go ahead of him.

Music was playing in the background and the lights were turned low. An afghan was draped over the back of the couch and the coffee table held a plant. Despite the boxes stacked along one wall, the room looked and felt cozy and welcoming.

"I know it looks like I'm settling in for the long haul," Claire said, apologetic as she set the tray on the low coffee table. "But my mom and sister insisted that I make the place look homey."

"Fine by me," Nik said, lowering himself to the couch opposite the easy chair he guessed was the one Claire sat in. A throw lay over its back and the table beside it held an assortment of books.

Either her or her family had also strung curtains on the abandoned curtain rods and hung up a few pictures.

She poured him his coffee then sat down in her chair, curling her feet up under her. Her hair hung loose, spilling over her shoulders, gleaming in the half-light of the room.

They were quiet for a moment, as if unsure what to say.

Nik wanted to ask about her plans, but he didn't want to pressure her and he guessed she didn't want to hear about his plans.

"Does Emma enjoy playing baseball?" he finally asked, thankful to find an easy discussion topic.

Claire tilted her hand in a gesture of uncertainty. "Not really. She doesn't feel like she's very good at it."

"It's not a pre-cursor to the big leagues," he joked, settling back in his chair.

"No. But she is a perfectionist. Curse of being an oldest or in her case, an only, child."

"You sound like you know what that's like. Are you the oldest?"

Claire took a sip of her coffee. "Yep. And I'm also a perfectionist. But what I've struggled the hardest with is being a people pleaser. I heard that was an oldest child's thing too. Did you have that problem?"

"I like things done a certain way," he admitted. "As far as being a people pleaser, I think that was always part of my makeup."

A memory of sitting upstairs, struggling with his math homework; carefully erasing mistakes so he wouldn't waste paper. Needing to get everything just perfect. Blended through the fear of being punished if he didn't get it right was an innate desire to earn some kind of praise from either his foster mother or father.

He never did.

"It's a hard thing to get rid of. The people pleasing as well as the perfectionist part," she said.

"Funny, I never pegged you for a people pleaser," Nik replied

"Oh, I've had my struggles there. I think I spent most of my life trying to make my mother happy. That got harder to do as I got older and then there was the whole unwed mother thing I dropped on her." Claire shrugged, her smile was a bit forced and Nik heard a faint note of pain in her voice. "But the perfectionist part. Yeah. That's totally me. When I set up the coffee shop, Tess kept telling me I should relax. That good enough was good enough."

"But good is the enemy of best," Nik returned, quoting one of his beloved foster mother's favorite maxims.

"Right?" She flashed him a smile—one much less superficial than the last; it reached her eyes. "Tess likes to deal with things as they come but I need a plan. We agree to disagree."

"You and Tess get along really well, don't you?"

Claire smiled again. "I'm thankful that we're back together in the same town. She's my sister but she's also my best friend."

"I remember that about the two of you."

"What do you mean, you remember?"

"I saw you two out and about once in a while."

"I thought you never went to school?" This netted him a puzzled frown.

"No. But sometimes I'd sneak out of the house. Walk around town. I'd see you and your sister together. I remember one time especially." He stopped there, realizing how that sounded. Like he had been stalking them.

"When was that?"

"Doesn't matter."

"I'd like to know," she pressed.

He thought for a moment, but figured he had nothing to lose by telling her. "It was in the park. Tess was walking on a narrow ledge and you were holding her hand, steadying her, warning her to be careful. Then she fell and landed on you. I thought for sure you would be angry, and she would be crying but you were both lying on the grass, laughing your heads off." He smiled at the memory of the girls lying side by side, helpless with giggles, laughing up at the sky. "It was neat to see."

"We did have a lot of fun together," Claire said, cradling her mug.

"You were lucky to have such a good relationship with your sister."

"You had siblings when you lived here, didn't you?"

"Yeah. The foster family I lived with had two of their own kids. A girl my age and a boy a year younger."

"Were they foster kids as well?"

"No. They were the Baleys' natural kids."

"And also homeschooled?"

"Yup."

"And you didn't get along with them?"

Nik took another sip of coffee, buying time as other memories invaded, trying to find a way to explain that wouldn't make him sound like he felt sorry for himself. "I wouldn't say we didn't get along, I just didn't spend much time with them."

Her frown showed her puzzlement. "How could you not? You lived in the same house."

"I spent a lot of time in my room."

"Ah. A recluse."

"Not often by choice." The words jumped out before he could stop them. Claire set her coffee cup down and leaned forward, her face puzzled.

"What are you saying?" She asked the question in a soft tone.

Nik wanted to stop there. He knew going back to that time would bring out emotions he couldn't control. He blamed it on the house. On being here and the mood it projected.

"That was in the past," he said, struggling to sound casual.

"Maybe, but I believe it's seeping into your present," Claire said.

Nik clenched his fist as he wrestled the memories back into submission.

Then to his surprise and dismay, Claire was sitting beside him, her hand on his shoulder.

"What happened here?" She asked. "You told me once you didn't have happy memories here, but I think it's worse than that."

He drew in a shuddering breath as frustration and anger surged through him. He couldn't tell her everything. "You wouldn't understand. You with your perfect life and your perfect family," he managed.

"My family is far from perfect. And my life is far from perfect. I'm living in someone else's house, the single mother of a six-year-old daughter. I would hardly call that a fairytale ending."

Nik felt ashamed. "You're right. And I'm sorry."

But she kept her hand where it was, and much as he knew he should pull away it had been so long since someone had tried to connect with him, had shown him even an ounce of sympathy, and he didn't want to move.

"So, what happened here?" she insisted.

Nik wove his fingers together, his hands so tight his knuckles turned white as pictures crowded to the forefront of his mind, clamoring to be released. Maybe it would help if he dumped them. Maybe.

"When I first moved in with the Baley family, I was about eight years old."

"But Cory said you were adopted out when you were four," she said.

"I was. But that adoption failed. And I got put into the foster system. That's how I ended up with the Baleys."

"That must've been so difficult for you."

"It was hard. Especially when I found out that the first couple who adopted me hoped taking in a child would fix a marriage that was falling apart. Guess it didn't work." He tried to inject a light tone into his voice, hoping he could show her he was over that. "Anyhow, I got into the Baley family when they lived in Lethbridge. It was okay at first. Then my foster father lost his job and we moved here. They insisted on home-schooling me and their children and that's when I found out how dysfunctional my foster parents actually were. It went okay at first, but slowly the cracks started showing. Nothing I did was ever good enough, I was a waste of time, I wasn't their kid, they weren't getting paid enough to take care of me." His knee bounced again, and he pushed his elbow down on it to stop it. He wasn't a kid anymore. He had to get over this.

"You said you spent a lot of time in your bedroom. Was that because you were sent there?"

She asked her questions quietly, gently probing. He wanted to resist, but then he looked into her eyes. The sympathy he saw there bothered him. He didn't like a woman feeling sorry for him.

And yet, at the same time, he saw concern.

"Were they abusive?" she asked, her voice quiet.

"Emotionally and physically." He ground the words out, wishing he could distance himself from that time.

"Why?"

Why indeed?

"I don't know, but nothing I ever did was good enough. No matter how hard I tried. And after a while, I stopped trying. And that's when things got really bad. I mouthed off to them. At first they would yell back, send me to my room. But things escalated each time." He sucked in a long, slow breath, struggling to slow down the pounding of his heart. He closed his eyes but that only made it worse. Again, he could feel the sting of a callused hand across his cheek. How his head would snap back when his foster father hit him extra hard. A boot to the shins and, if he fell down, an extra one to his ribs. "Things got physical."

"And all of this was happening while you lived here? Oh, Nik. I'm sorry. We never knew."

"No one knew. Rick was always very careful not to create bruises in places that would show. And if he did, off to my room I went until they healed. They had many ways of controlling me. Food was a big one. I spent so many years in this house hungry…" His voice trembled, and he fought the weakness into submission. He should stop now. He didn't want to go back into that darkness, but it was as if the words he'd held back so long demanded release. "I tried to run away a couple of times, but I always got caught and brought back here. Which started off another cycle of abuse and pain and hunger. Those little hidey-holes your daughter loves so much were, to me, a place of fear and terror. I'd be locked in there sometimes for days at a time."

Claire's hand tightened on his shoulder as the words spilled out. He struggled with the mixture of anger and even worse, sorrow. As a child he had shed enough tears and he wouldn't let that happen again. Not in front of Claire.

"I wish we'd known," she agreed. "I wish we'd

known what you were going through. I used to come by this house just to look at my old home, and sometimes I'd see you sitting on the deck. Should've come and talked to you. I should have been a better neighbor. I should have been a better Christian."

"How were you to know?" To his dismay the question came out through an ever-thickening throat. He swallowed and swallowed again. "No one knew what was going on in this house. Not even the cops who brought me back here every time. Or the social worker the few times that poor overworked woman would come for a visit."

"And you had nowhere to turn."

This sympathy in her voice was his undoing. A sob crawled up his throat followed by another. He squeezed his eyes shut, clenched his hands tighter as his shoulders shook with silent grief. He hadn't cried since he ended up in Rebecca Huizinga's home and he didn't want to now. Not in front of this woman who was growing more appealing to him.

"Oh Nik," Claire said. "What you have had to deal with is unspeakable. I'm so sorry we didn't help you. I'm so sorry we didn't pay attention."

And then her arms were around him, holding him close.

He wanted to push her back; he wasn't a child anymore. He was a man, and he didn't need sympathy from a woman.

But he didn't pull away. Couldn't. Her comfort filled the empty places in him that he'd tried to fill with more work, more holidays, more of whatever he thought would make the ache of it go away.

It never did.

He slipped his arms around her, swallowing his grief.

Then, to his dismay, she brushed a kiss over his cheek.

And another sob slipped past his reserve. He struggled to fight it into submission but the hunger in him yearned for the closeness Claire offered. Comfort he was now receiving from this amazing and wonderful woman.

He pressed his hands against his face, still fighting but the sobs came faster now. And she held him even closer. Pictures flashed through his mind, each creating more pain and anguish. His mother leaving him, the Jensen's leaving him, his foster father beating him. He couldn't let the memories win but the pain took over and the tears flowed.

After what seemed like an eternity, he finally fought the sorrow into submission.

He tried to pull back from Claire as he regained control.

But she wouldn't let him move away. She cradled his face in her hands her eyes gentle on him. "I wish I could tell you how sorry I am. I apologize that we did not help you. That you had to suffer this all alone."

Nik held her gaze, heard the sincerity in her voice, her hands gentle on his face. He felt as if he should man up, take control but other emotions flitted over her face. She was about to remove her hands when he caught them in his own, curling his fingers through hers.

"Like I said, how were you to know if the people who were supposed to protect me didn't? Wouldn't?" He swallowed, drawing in a shaky breath, thankful his emotions were falling back into line.

She looked at their interlocked hands. "I understand why this house doesn't make you happy."

Her admission surprised him but also validated his feelings and his plans.

"So, you know why I have to get rid of it?"

"Maybe." She lifted her eyes to his and he

could see pain in them. "But I remember laughter and fun and joy and a family that enjoyed being together. It was a good home for me and my family. It was the best place I ever lived in. That happened in this house too."

"I need to move on," he said quietly, struggling with his conflicting emotions. "And I don't think I can do that until this place is gone."

"But it's just a building," she replied.

"I could say the same to you."

She blinked again, and, to his surprise, dislodged a tear.

Now it was his turn to comfort her as he held her face and thumbed the tear away. But he let his hand linger, stroking her face. His breath quickened as their eyes held and then he didn't want to talk anymore.

All the lingering glances they had shared the past few weeks, the memories he had harbored of her, the attraction he knew was growing blended in this moment.

He leaned closer, their breath mingling for a heartbeat.

Stifling doubts, second thoughts and warnings, he gave in to his yearnings, leaned in closer and kissed her.

Her lips were warm and soft and inviting. He

slipped his arms around her, drawing her closer as their kiss deepened. She wrapped her arms around his, her mouth moving over his.

Her fingers caressed his face, slipping over his cheeks, his chin, as if memorizing his features.

Too quickly she drew back but kept her forehead pressed against his, her eyes downcast. He couldn't make out her features and didn't want to catch her reaction. But she didn't move out of his embrace.

And he wasn't apologizing for his impulse.

It felt right to have her in his arms, her slight body pressed against his. It felt like they were both exactly where they were should be.

Her breath feathered over his mouth and while he wanted to kiss her again, he also sensed she needed a moment to absorb what had just happened.

So did he.

Then she slowly leaned back in his embrace, a question in the depths of her eyes.

Curbing his own questions about what they were doing and where they were going, he kissed her again.

When he leaned back on the couch she came with him, curling up against him, one arm around him, her hand resting on his chest. He laid his cheek against her hair, releasing a long held, deep sigh. He closed his eyes, shutting out the house, letting the classical music Claire had playing on the stereo soothe the harsh feelings. Letting him simply enjoy holding this amazing woman in his arms.

Her fingers made circles on his chest, their gentle movement easing away the tension that always gripped him when he came in the house.

"I'm glad you did that," she said, her voice soft, a gentle murmur. "Kissed me."

"I am too." He pressed a light kiss on her head and eased out another sigh. "Something I've wanted to do for a long time."

"What do you mean, 'a long time?'" She pulled back at that, frowning in her puzzlement. "You've only been here a couple of weeks."

"This time around." He fingered a strand of hair away from her face, wondering what she would think when he told her. "I would see you in town, like that time I saw you with Tess. I liked watching you biking around town. You always looked so carefree and happy."

"I was biking to get out of the house. My parents were probably fighting, and I wanted to be free. So I'd come and either bike or walk past this place."

"I remember that. There were lots of times I'd be in my room in this house, sitting at my desk. I was supposed to be working and I would see you stop on the sidewalk and look at the house."

"That means you were staying in either my mom's sewing room or my dad's study. Those are the only rooms that look out over the street."

"It was the one on the north end of the house."

"My mom's sewing room then. It was tiny." And then her face grew serious. "And it had a couple of cubby holes in it. The ones that Emma loves hiding in."

He nodded, his heart starting up again.

"Were you locked in them?"

He gave her another nod.

Claire closed her eyes, as if she didn't want to acknowledge that.

He wanted to comfort her. To assure her that those events were another part of his life.

But that would be hypocritical.

Breaking down in her arms had released an army of memories, marching through his brain, relentless. Take no prisoners.

He wanted them gone.

And he knew the only way that would happen was if he razed this house to the ground. Burying the memories and destroying the place they dwelled.

Once that was done, he could finally be released from that humiliating and painful part of his past.

* * *

A DOOR SLAMMED UPSTAIRS, and Claire jumped away from Nik.

"I think that's Emma," Claire said, her voice trembling with the emotions that still raced through her.

She got up, smoothing her hair, struggling with a guilt she didn't want to feel.

"Mommy," Emma called out. "I'm thirsty."

"Just stay up there. I'll bring you some water," Claire returned hoping her cheeks weren't as red as they felt. She shot Nik a warning glance. But his head was down, and she hesitated, wondering what he was thinking.

As she walked past him to the kitchen, she blamed her impulse on loneliness, and the fact that a man had broken down in front of her. Had shown weakness. Had shed tears.

That had never happened to her before. And even though she had felt sad for him, that emotion shifted to a whole different one as he kissed her.

She pressed her hands to her heated cheeks, then opened a packing box on the table and pulled a glass out. She hadn't wanted to put too many things in the cupboard, knowing she would have to pack up again once she found a place to stay. Though it had only been a couple of days, living out of the boxes was getting boring. And a stark reminder of how tenuous her life was. No house to buy, no apartment to return to. The future was a foggy place of uncertainty.

She fought down a beat of fear as she filled Emma's glass from a pitcher in the fridge.

Dear Lord, please let me trust in you. Please let me know you are watching over us. Help me to trust you will get us through this.

Her parents had always taught her to bring everything to God in prayer. This was how she got through those dark days after Andy left her high and dry with a three-month-old baby and she had to find a way to make it on her own. But lately it seemed even her prayers were agitated, creating more ambivalence than comfort.

She took a deep breath and turned.

"I always get thirsty when I'm lying in bed," Claire heard Emma say.

The little stinker had come downstairs anyways.

Claire walked into the living room and sure enough there was Emma, perched on the edge of the coffee table, her hands on her hips in her I'm-so-cool pose.

"I heard Mr. Nik talking, and I wanted to say hello," Emma said, her eyes wide, the picture of innocence.

"Well, you've said hello, now I want you to scoot back upstairs," Claire said, her tone firm.

"Are you coming to the church picnic on Saturday?" Emma asked, ignoring her mother, eyes focused on Nik.

It was as if she knew she held power and was wielding it.

"I didn't know there was a church picnic," Nik said. He leaned back in his seat, one ankle rested on his knee, looking surprisingly comfortable considering what had just happened. He was smiling.

"It will be so fun," Emma said. "We're having races, and contests. I baked some cookies for it, even."

"Oh, and here I thought they were for me," Nik said with a laugh.

"Yes, they were for you, but they were also for

the picnic." Emma's quick recovery was admirable and before Claire could reprimand her, Emma continued, shooting a pleading look Claire's way. "I really want Mr. Nik to come to the picnic. All the other kids will bring their dads and I don't have a dad."

And here we go again. It was time to stop that line of conversation.

"Here's your drink and then it's bedtime, missy," Claire warned.

"But I'm not tired," Emma whined. "Can we play a game?" Before Claire could protest, Emma ran to another packing box and lifted the flaps. She pulled another box out and brought it back to the coffee table, setting it down. "I like playing Chinese checkers, and I just learned how to do it. I'm not very good at it, so you can help me."

She was doing this on purpose, Claire realized. Pushing back in front of Nik; forcing Claire's hand. Short of grabbing Emma by the arm and dragging her up the stairs, Claire was stuck. And after what Nik had just told her, she wasn't using physical force on her daughter.

"We can play one game," Claire conceded. "But then you have to go back to bed."

Emma's grin went from ear to ear. Claire

knew she had lost some authority, but she wasn't engaging in public battle with her daughter.

Emma set the box on the table and lifted the lid, explaining the directions to Nik. She looked up at Claire, "You can just put my glass of water beside me," she said.

"Yes, boss." Claire rolled her eyes and set it down then knelt beside her daughter resting her elbows on the table and looking directly at Emma. "Just one game, remember?" she warned. She was giving in, but sensed Emma knew not to push back too hard.

Emma agreed and pulled the marbles out. She handed one pile to Nik, laid out one for herself and then gave her mother hers.

"I'll just watch," Claire said. Playing with the three of them would extend the game.

"Please, Mommy? We hardly ever get to play games together." The pathos in her voice made it sound like Claire seldom did anything with her daughter. So, with a stifled sigh, she gave in. Again.

She blamed her slack discipline on the tangle of their lives the past few days. Hard to find a rhythm when you didn't know which direction you were marching.

"You aren't allowed to take my marble when

you jump it like you do in checkers or chess," Emma warned Nik.

"You know how to play chess?" Nik sounded impressed.

"It's really easy," Emma pronounced as she set the marbles out.

"We play our own version," Claire said, catching Nik's surprise.

"Ah. I see." His surprise turned to a smile and once again she couldn't look away.

As their gaze lengthened her breath quickened and she felt as if her lips were still warm from his kiss.

"You can move first," Emma said looking from Claire to Nik, breaking the moment.

"Of course," Claire said, ignoring her daughter's puzzled look and moving a marble out.

Soon the game was underway.

"This is so fun," Emma crowed as she hopped over Nik's marbles which, Claire suspected, he had laid out precisely for her. "I think I will win."

"Which would be awesome," Claire said, following Nik's lead and setting Emma up. The sooner this game was over the sooner her daughter would be back in bed and not discussing dads and fathers in front of Nik.

"Why are you doing that?" Emma challenged her. "That move doesn't make any sense."

Looked like her daughter was on to her. "I'm going to jump over Nik's marbles," she said. "Your turn now."

"Let's see, let's see." Emma tapped her chin as she decided which move to make. Claire was about to encourage her to do something when Emma hopped her marble all the way across the board then smiled up at Nik. "So, Mr. Nik did you think about the church picnic? I think you should come. It's a lot of fun."

Claire should have known Emma wouldn't let this go. "Mr. Nik probably has other plans," she said, trying to catch Emma's eye.

"Do you?" Emma asked him as she danced her marble across the board and into her home slot. "Have other plans?"

"I have a few things I need to organize the next few days," Nik replied moving his marble.

Claire suppressed her panic, guessing the things he needed to organize had to do with the house.

"But you don't have plans on Saturday?" Emma pressed.

"No. Not really."

"You could totally come," Emma crowed, clapping her hands. "The picnic is on Saturday and my mom is getting Aunty Tess to work in the cafe and Saturday is usually off for people." Before Nik could reply Emma turned to Claire, her eyes wide. "Maybe Mr. Nik can buy your basket. That would be so cool. We could sit all together and eat it." She spun back to Nik, a conversational dervish, Claire couldn't stop. "I would love that. Last year my mommy and I sat by with my grandpa and gramma because my grandpa bought my mom's basket and that wasn't as much fun."

"I think that's enough about the picnic," Claire interjected before her daughter could say anything else. "You're making Mr. Nik uncomfortable." Claire shot her daughter a stern glance. Thankfully, this time, Emma took the hint. She looked down, her smile fading.

"I just don't want Billy Dansworth to poke fun of me again," she mumbled.

"Billy pokes fun of everyone," Claire said making her move. "And you should learn to ignore him."

"But he's so mean. The other day he told my friends at school that I didn't have a dad because I was so ugly. I'm not ugly, am I?" This question was directed to Nik as if Emma knew what

Claire's response would be. Clearly, she needed a second opinion.

"I think you're a fun girl who is very attractive," Nik returned.

"Does that mean I'm pretty?"

"It means you're pretty amazing," Nik parried.

Claire had to chuckle at his deft responses.

"But I want to be pretty, pretty. You know, beautiful," Emma said.

"My foster mother used to say that 'grace is deceitful, and beauty is vain'. So, it's really not important to be beautiful."

Emma frowned as if trying to figure out what he was saying. "So what's a foster mother? Is that different than a regular mother?"

Of all the things Nik had just told her, Claire did not think her daughter would land on that particular item. "A foster mother is someone who helps kids who don't have a family," Claire put in, sparing Nik the need to reply. "And you need to make a move missy."

"You don't have a family, Mr. Nik?" Emma's frown deepened as she hopped her marble down the board.

Claire held in a groan. She thought she had helped Nik, instead she had created more questions for Emma.

"I actually do," Nik said. "Your baseball coach, Cory, is my sister."

"Did Miss Cory have a foster mother, too?"

At that Nik's smile slid into a dark frown. "And now I'm making an epic jump," he said, evading her question.

Clearly Emma had stepped into territory Nik didn't want to discuss as he made his move.

"So did she?" Emma asked.

"We need to finish up this game," Claire said, reaching over and giving her daughter's arm a warning squeeze. "Bedtime isn't going away."

"Okay, but I still think I will win," Emma said.

"I think so, too." Claire gave her daughter a gentle smile, then stroked the arm she had just squeezed. "You're a good player."

"I know you guys let me win," she said matter-of-factly as she moved her last marble into place. "And that's okay. I like winning."

"Isn't that a fact." Claire tempered her comment with another smile her daughter's way. It seemed Emma was more perceptive than she gave her credit for.

"And if Mr. Nik comes to the church picnic than maybe you can finally win the three-legged race," Emma said, gathering up the marbles. "Last year, you and Miss Cory were way behind and I don't think Auntie Tess will be much help because she will probably want to race with Uncle Jace. So what should we do about that?"

Whatever would she do with this girl?

"Nothing at all," Claire said, getting up and taking the game from her daughter. "And now the evening is over for you."

Emma looked like she wanted to say something more, but this time Claire took her hand grasping it firmly in hers. "Say goodnight to Mr. Nik," she said.

"Goodnight Mr. Nik," Emma said, her voice subdued. "I sure hope you can come to the picnic."

Claire tugged on Emma's arm and escorted her upstairs. Thankfully Emma went along with no protest.

She tucked her daughter in and sat on the bed to give her a mini lecture about her behavior concerning Nik. Emma suddenly sat up and grabbed Claire by the neck. "I'm so sad, Mommy." She sniffled.

Claire wrapped her arms around her daughter, pulling her close. "What are you sad about, honey?"

"I don't want to move out of the house."

Neither do I.

"But it's not our house, honey. It's Mr. Nik's now. And we'll find another nice place to live."

"But there won't be a yard for Mooch to play in," Emma complained. "And I don't want to live in another apartment."

Claire gently released Emma's arms and sat back, still holding her daughter's hands. "You know what's the most important thing, don't you?" Claire asked.

"That we love Jesus with all our heart?"

"Absolutely, that is the most important thing," Claire said with a smile. "Do you know what's the second most important thing?" she amended.

"That we love each other?"

"You got it. And because we love each other so much, it doesn't matter where we live. We will always be together, you and me."

"Will I ever get a dad?"

Claire bit back a sigh at her daughter's persistence but kept her cool and kept her response simple.

"We have each other. We don't need a dad to be happy." Claire's thoughts shifted back to Andy and the struggle she went through with him after they were married.

Lance had often spoken of his mother and how she dominated his life. How he struggled with the pain. Claire knew Andy had a difficult family life and she foolishly thought she could love the pain away. But he never got past it. Could never stop talking about it. If anything, he grew more bitter with each month they lived together.

Then came the day that he decided to leave. He confronted her, accusing her of being like his mother. Trying to dominate him. Tying him down. Told her how much he hated the feeling. That he needed to be free. He couldn't let go of the pain and he couldn't even begin to consider her and Emma's needs.

And on the heels of that degrading memory came the few dates she did dare go on. Dates not repeated once the guys found out that she had a daughter. She knew those words and actions shouldn't haunt or define her but they sunk into the pit that seemed to inhabit her life, that place of low self-esteem.

But there's a man downstairs who kissed you. Who seems interested in you. Who is good with Emma.

A man who is leaving once he's done here.

"I would still like a dad," Emma said, pulling her hands away from Claire and folding them over her stomach. "And I will keep praying for one."

That Claire couldn't do anything about, and while a small part of her sometimes thought the same, she knew from experience that she and Emma were better off on their own.

* * *

NIK GOT up from the couch, restless, not sure what to make of what had just happened. Trying to sort Emma's comments from his kiss. Trying to put it all in its proper place.

He had some breathing space to think about it now that Emma and Claire were gone.

Thinking of his breakdown in front of Claire made him squirm. How had he let that happen?

He pulled in a deep breath, old emotions battling with new. A memory of himself sitting in his room upstairs, arms wrapped around his knees, jaw clenched in a combination of fear and fury. Promising himself he would never cry again.

All it had taken was one beautiful woman and a heavy dose of tangible sympathy and his promise faded like frost in the sun.

Even now, after the storm of sorrow and the joy of kissing Claire, anger prowled at the edges of his consciousness like a dark, malevolent beast, waiting to pounce and dig its claws in him. He tried to shake it off. Tried to relive that glorious moment, holding Claire in his arms, feeling as if his world had found a calm and quiet center.

And now that woman was upstairs putting her child to bed in a house that haunted him.

He swallowed again, clenching and unclenching his fists as he looked around the living room. The boxes piled in one corner, the worn furniture, the soft lighting created a different atmosphere than the dank darkness he had always associated with this place. Even hearing Claire's soft murmuring from upstairs as she put Emma to bed seemed to ease his bleak thoughts.

He knew he should go, but he wanted to wait until Claire came down the stairs, so he could say a proper goodbye.

And kiss her again?

He squeezed his eyes closed, still not sure where to put everything. How to sort it all out. He was getting involved with a woman who had the potential to throw his world upside down. To make him change his plans.

And why not?

The three words swirled through all the other words and emotions, shifting and rearranging them.

He shook his head. He had a plan and if there

was one thing life had taught him it was to stick to your plans. Don't let other people determine your life's path. This had happened to him too many times.

Finally, he heard a door close and footsteps down the hall. As soon as Claire came down the stairs her eyes met his and the relief on her face was evident. As if she were wondering whether he would leave while she was gone.

"I thought I would stick around and say goodbye," Nik said, slipping his hands in the back pockets of his jeans, not sure he trusted himself to get too close to Claire.

"I'm sorry about Emma and her comments. She's been out of sorts lately."

"Understandable. Your life has been tossed topsy-turvy the past few days." As his had in the past few hours.

Claire slipped her fingers through her hair.

Nik took a breath. "I want to say I'm sorry—"

"Emma was just being—"

They spoke at the same time and when he saw the hurt retreat in her eyes, in how she wrapped her arms around her midsection. She must think he was apologizing for kissing her when he wanted to apologize for breaking down in her arms.

But as his senses overtook his emotions, he realized this might be a good thing. He needed to back off, create some space.

"Thanks again for fixing the smoke detector," she said, her eyes fixed on her hands.

For a moment he wanted to cross the room. To explain.

However, maybe it was better this way.

Yet, as he left, closing the door behind him, walking toward his darkened, empty trailer, he couldn't seem to convince himself that he should have said something.

CHAPTER 8

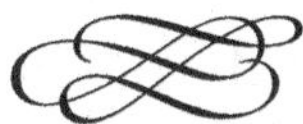

"No, Chance. I haven't changed my mind about the house." Nik said, fiddling with the volume of the Bluetooth, fighting his second thoughts.

Chance had first called when he was signing a contract with a track hoe operator whom he'd hired to tear-down the house after his other operator had bailed on him. Nik had ignored the call, but when he got into the truck and started driving and Chance called again, he connected the call through his truck's wireless connection. He was just driving, anyway. May as well talk.

"Just thought I'd check. You seemed a little uncertain last time we chatted."

"Chatted? Seriously? You been watching girly

movies again?" Nik chose to deflect rather than let his friend find even the smallest crack in his defenses. Chance was relentless in his desire to see Nik settle down.

"You could do with a few more chick flicks in your life. Help you get in touch with your softer side."

"What can I do for you, buddy?" Nik said, getting to the point.

"Don't tear down the house."

Relentless.

"Well, I just spent all day yesterday and this morning lining up trucks and track hoes after my other contractor bailed on me, so that would be a no."

"Bailed on you? When did that happen?"

"Thursday night." After he had kissed Claire and then fought with regrets and concerns. "And this guy won't be able to start for at least three weeks."

"That's interesting. Did you ever get the feeling that these delays are happening for a reason?"

"God intervening in my life?" Nik couldn't keep the sardonic tone from his voice.

"Why not?"

"Because He never did before."

Chance was quiet a moment. "He brought you into Mrs. Huizinga's place. He gave you a healthy body and the ability to make a living. A good living, I might add."

Nik had to concede that point.

"And He brought you back together with your mother and sister."

"A mother who gave me up, but not her daughter."

Another moment of quiet followed his outburst. Nik slowed down, making the long turn onto the road leading to Sweet Creek.

"Sounds to me, from what you've told me, that she was in a tight spot. I'm sure she didn't do it because she didn't love you. I'm sure she did it because she *did*."

Chance's reasonable words slipped in behind the anger that Nik had held onto for so long, nudging at it. His anger had defined his relationship with his mother. But every time he saw his mother face-to-face, that anger was harder to hold on to.

"I have to think of a quote from Psalms," Chance said. "'Can a mother forget the child of her womb?' Or something like that. The fact that your mother held on to Cory and did what she could to keep her, shows that she probably regrets what she did with you. And if she had even had a chance, she would've kept you too."

Nik held that thought for a moment, letting it settle as he eased out another sigh.

"She was happy to see you, wasn't she?"

"Not the first time."

"Guilt is a hard thing to bear," Chance said. "But they went looking for you, so I'm thinking she's been struggling with guilt and regret this whole time. That can't be easy for her."

His comments gave Nik more to mull over.

"I don't think you need to make this complicated," Chance continued. "Allow yourself to see her as a broken human being who did the best she could. I know, deep down, you care about her, otherwise you wouldn't feel so strongly about your perception of her giving you up for adoption."

"See, this is why I keep you as my friend," Nik said. "You put things into perspective."

"Speaking of perspective, how are things with you and Claire?"

"I don't see how the two are connected," Nik said.

Though having the other contractor quit on him was a royal pain, he was thankful for the busyness it created. Rustling up a new contractor had kept him away from Claire and her precocious daughter the past couple of days. The kiss he had shared with Claire haunted him every waking minute.

He swallowed again, reliving that moment, that feeling of utter rightness he had never felt with anybody else.

"Not connected at all," Chance said. "But I couldn't find a smoother way to segue from one into the other."

"The only thing I'll say is that it's complicated."

"This is a conversation, not an update on your Facebook status."

"She has a kid," Nik said. "So that makes it complicated. I can't just waltz in and out of her life. It's not fair to Emma."

"Then don't waltz out," Chance said. "Stick around."

Nik tapped his fingers on the steering wheel, reason fighting with the lonely and yearning part of him that wanted to see Claire again. Wanted to spend time with her.

"I wish it were that easy," Nik said.

"Don't over analyze this," Chance said. "Sometimes it's okay to decide with your heart, not your head."

“Thanks for the tip,” Nik said. "I'll take it under advisement."

“And while you're doing that, once again, I'll be praying for you."

“I do appreciate that," Nik finally said. "One of these days, I should do that for myself."

“No time like the present," Chance said with a chuckle.

Nik was about to answer with some smart remark to lighten the mood, when a number flashed on the console of the truck showing another call coming in. Cory.

“Sorry, Chance. I have to take another call.”

“Popular guy this morning,” Chance said. “Take care and, like I said, don’t think about this too much. Be responsible but allow yourself some happiness.”

“That’s a contradiction if ever I heard one. But I’ll try.” He hit a button on his steering wheel to disconnect the call and connect with his sister.

“Hey Cory, how are you?” he said.

“Good. Catch you at a good time?”

“Just driving. Had to do a bunch of running around.”

“For the house?” Her hopeful tone made him feel guilty. The last time they spoke, she had offered to help him paint. He had smiled and thanked her, unable to tell her the truth about his long-term plans.

"Yeah," was all he said, again being intentionally vague.

"It was good to see you at baseball practice the other day," she said, the warmth in her voice coming through the phone. "It made me feel so good to have actual family around. Hasn't happened before."

"I know what that feels like," he said. "So yeah, it was fun for me, too."

"I feel like I'm constantly invading your life."

"That's okay. You're my sister." He smiled as he spoke those words. "I've never had a sister before."

"But you had a foster sister?"

"Not really." He couldn't go back there so soon. Not after practically crying in Claire's arms. The memory brought a mixture of shame that he had been so weak, yet it also produced a feeling of peace. Of coming home.

The irony of this happening in the place he least considered home wasn't lost on him.

"We can delve into that later," Cory said. "I wanted to see if you are busy this afternoon. I know I should have called sooner, but my brain hasn't been functioning well the past few days."

"Too much wedding planning?"

"Something like that. Anyhow, Matthew, Mom and I are going to the church picnic and we'd love it if you could come. It starts at 5:00 and will be at the main park just off Main Street, across from City Hall. But if you want supper, bring your wallet. There's a basket auction."

"Are you making one?"

"Well, yeah," she spoke as if this were a foregone conclusion.

"Let me guess, you want me to come so I bid on yours in case Matthew doesn't," he teased.

"That might be a consideration. I should warn Matthew he might have a contender." She chuckled, and the sound warmed another lonely part of Nik's soul. Their easy give and take surprised him. They barely knew each other and yet she was comfortable to be around. Biology truly created a connection which was difficult to explain. "Anyhow, it's just a casual event. Might be a good time for you to re-connect with Mom. I know the last visit was kinda tense."

"It was hard to find out that Mom kept you and gave me up." His words sounded harsh, but he couldn't stop the truth.

Another beat of silence followed his admission.

"She told you the reasons."

"Which explains what happened to her but didn't help me much." He pressed his lips together as he fought other emotions. He'd never had a hard time keeping them under control before. But since he met his mother and Cory and since Claire, it was getting harder.

"I'm sure it didn't," she said, her voice quietly understanding. "And I wish we could change that."

"It's done," he said. Abandonment was something he'd been dealing with for many years. Rebecca took him for counselling, which helped him identify the issue. He thought by doing that he'd put it behind him, but his reaction to his mother's story made him realize what a joke that was.

Allow yourself to think of her as a broken human being.

Chance's words returned, creating a flurry of other emotions.

"We would like to see you again," Cory continued. "Please consider coming. If not for Mom, then for me. You don't have to spend the whole time with us. Even just a few moments would be nice."

"I'll think about it."

Apparently, she wasn't the only one hoping he would show up. He had to smile as he thought of Emma's blatant appeal for him to attend.

"Okay. That's all I can ask for. We have to leave, so maybe we'll see you there."

He said goodbye as the truck swooped down the hill and over the river into town. He turned off and drove down Main Street, slowing as he passed the two and three-story brick buildings with their moldings and fancy windows. Wrought iron lampposts curled over the street. Flowers, still blooming, hung from hooks below the lights. Benches flanked by flower pots dotted the brick sidewalks. Each corner of the street also held large brick planters overflowing with purple, pink and white petunias.

His foster mother would have loved this place. He appreciated what the town had done to maintain an old-world beauty without succumbing to kitsch.

Nice place to live, he thought, slowing suddenly as a young boy rolled across the street on a skateboard, licking on an ice cream cone as his dog pulled him along. The boy waved nonchalantly at Nik, clearly unperturbed by the fact that he held Nik up. Despite his minor annoyance, Nik smiled back. His smile grew more genuine when the boy stopped on the other side of the street to talk to a group of young girls.

He remembered walking down these streets the few times he'd sneaked out of the house. It was often quieter when the stores were closed but the Riverside Inn was open, as were a few pubs. He would saunter down the sidewalk, as if he belonged there, his heart pounding each time he heard someone call out. The penalty for his momentary freedom would be hard and swift, but only if he were caught. So he made sure he wasn't.

He made another turn down a winding street that followed the river.

As he got closer to the house, the old familiar dread seeped into his veins. He sucked in a deep breath as he parked his truck on the driveway.

Claire's car was gone. Probably at the picnic.

Nik shut the engine off, staring at his trailer. The thought of going in there and eating supper by himself held no appeal. Nor did going out for supper by himself.

There's the picnic.

Cory wanted him to come. Emma wanted him to come.

And he would see Claire again.

Drumming his fingers, he considered his options. Spend time with people or sit and brood in an empty trailer?

Be alone or possibly see Claire?

Before he could change his mind, he started up the truck again, backed out of the driveway and headed back to the park.

He parked his truck a couple of blocks away because there were so many vehicles. He wondered how popular a church picnic could be. Turned out; very.

Thankfully the weather was balmy. Sun shone and a few

leaves that had already changed skittered across the road in front of him. Soon they would all be yellow and orange. He looked up to the mountains that protected the town, remembering how they glowed like they were lit from within when the aspen and poplar trees changed color. And then, later, how snow blanketed the harsh rock, softening the edges, sharply delineating the snowy peaks against a blue sky. The times he had snuck out and walked around, he could not keep his eyes off the mountains sheltering the town, wishing things were different for him. Wishing he were staying with another family so he could enjoy being here.

In his meanderings he would sometimes walk

past the school, wondering if he would see Claire. Occasionally he did but she never seemed to notice him.

The confusing memories, some good, some bad, blended with each other as he walked closer to the park, still thinking of Claire. He heard music and people talking, someone was speaking over an intercom system.

"So, we got another basket for your consideration," the announcer said.

Sounded like the auction had started and, as Nik got closer, he saw some people sitting by tables, already eating and others waiting, gathered around a large gazebo in the middle of the park.

He stayed on the edge, looking over the crowd, trying to find Cory.

Or Claire.

"Hello there. Are you visiting?" A woman with long, blonde hair, and a baby carrier over one arm stopped by his side.

"Is it that obvious?" Nik shifted his stance, shoving his hands in his pockets.

"You looked like you weren't sure where to go. Do you want a guide?" She angled her head toward the crowd. "Just follow me."

He was about to protest, still not certain he wanted to be there, but it would be rude to ignore her. So he followed her past the overhanging trees to the open space now filled with people.

"By the way, my name is Sheryl Andrews. That's my husband, Mark, handing the baskets to the auctioneer." She flashed him a teasing smile. "In case you thought I was coming on to you."

"Thanks for that."

"I know you single guys." She grinned again, holding up the baby car seat. "This is a guaranteed romance killer."

He frowned, unsure what to make of her comment.

"Sorry. I'm feeling feisty," she said, sensing his discomfort. "We just found out that little Nathaniel here won't need the surgery the doctors had been warning us about, so I'm on top of the world babbling to anyone who will listen."

"Oh. I see." He wasn't sure what to say to that except, "Congratulations. That's good news."

"I know. Oversharing with a stranger," she said. "But we are just so pleased. Such an answer to prayer. There's nothing like knowing your child will be okay to put a spring in a mother's step."

And no sooner had she spoken then he saw his own mother heading toward them. She was walking on her own, her eyes locked on him.

As Cory smiled and waved, Sheryl's gaze bounced between them and him. "I'm glad, for Joyce's sake, that you came here to see her." Sheryl sighed. "You are so fortunate to have your mother in your life. Mine died when I was young. I still miss her."

Her words only added another layer of unwelcome guilt. He didn't want to be reminded of his angry reunion with his mother and how he should be thankful to have her back in his life. Right now, he preferred to think about Claire and how being with her filled the lonely spaces in his soul.

"Sheryl, nice to see you," Cory said as she and Joyce joined them. "How is little Nathaniel doing?"

"Healthy as a horse, so we're thankful."

Cory lifted the blanket covering the baby carrier and smiled down at the baby. He gurgled and kicked his feet, the picture of health.

"He's so adorable," Cory said.

"You have to say that." Sheryl grinned. "But Mark and I think so and that's all that counts."

"But he is," Joyce put in, looking down at him, her smile melancholy. "Children are a precious gift."

Nik couldn't stop his thoughts from sifting

back. Was she thinking about when he was a baby? Wasn't he a precious gift for her?

I didn't want to give you up... I thought it was the best thing.

Joyce's anguished words slipped into his mind and as she looked over at him, he caught the glint of tears in her eyes. And he couldn't help an answering throb of his heart, an echo of his own pain.

Allow yourself to see her as a broken human being.

"We should all walk down to the auction," Sheryl said, flipping the blanket over the carrier again, a small tent for her son, breaking the tense moment.

"Good idea. We don't want Nik missing out on buying that special basket," Cory said, giving him a cheeky smile.

"Will he give Matthew a run for his money?" Sheryl asked.

"Maybe. Or he might bid on Claire's."

"Claire's?" Sheryl's curious gaze flicked from Cory to Nik.

No one spoke for a moment and Cory shot him an apologetic look. "Sorry. Slipped out."

"Interesting," was all Sheryl said, a cheeky smile slipping across her mouth. She looked like she wanted to say more but they were close to the gazebo now and her husband was calling her to come over.

"Sorry. Gotta go. You all take care," she said, fluttering her fingers at them and walking toward the gazebo, the baby carrier resting on her hip.

Cory turned to Nik, looking contrite. "Sorry about what I said in front of Sheryl. She's discreet. I don't think she'll say anything to anyone."

"It's okay." He had nothing else to say. He didn't want to talk about Claire in front of his sister or Joyce.

"Anyhow, we're sitting over there," Cory said, pointing to a grove of trees, where a few other people already had chairs out.

He walked alongside them, surprised Joyce could keep up. The last time he saw her she looked as if she couldn't sit up, let alone walk.

"You seem better today, Joyce," he said as she sat down in the lawn chairs Cory had set out.

"I feel a lot better." She gave him a tentative smile, as if uncertain of his response. Which made Nik think of what Chance had told him. He returned her smile.

Just love her.

So he reached over and laid his hand over hers, tightening his grip. And when her smile blossomed, so did something deep within him.

And when he noticed Claire and Emma sitting just a few feet ahead of him, a tiny glimmer of other possibilities grew as well.

* * *

"HE'S THE CUTEST BABY EVER," Emma proclaimed as Claire knelt down on the quilt Sheryl had spread out and lifted the blanket up from the baby carrier Sheryl Andrews had set on the ground beside her.

"He is adorable," Claire agreed, smiling over at Sheryl.

"You're talking to a very biased mother," Sheryl said, stroking his tiny head with a gentle hand.

"Was I ever that little?" Emma asked.

"Yes. Hard to believe you were." Claire felt a momentary pang of envy as she watched Emma coo over the baby. Claire had always wanted a large family. Kids born close together. A stairstep family.

Now Emma was six and there wasn't much chance of her getting siblings any time soon.

"Mommy. Look. Nik is here," Emma said, clapping her hands as she stood. "He came."

Claire kept her eyes on Nathanial, though she

wanted nothing more than to turn her head to see where Nik was. A flush warmed her cheeks as she thought of the kiss they had shared and how after that, he'd left and didn't return.

And now he was here, creating a peculiar lift of her heart.

"I'm going to talk to him," Emma said. But Claire caught her arm as she scrambled to her feet.

"Leave him alone," Claire said. If he wanted to see them, he could come to her. No way was she chasing after some guy.

"But he's just sitting with his mom and Cory."

The momentary joy she felt at his arrival was quashed. Of course. He wasn't here to see her. He only came for his mother and sister.

"I could tell him to come and join us," Sheryl said, giving Claire a sly smile. "I was just talking to him. I think Cory and Joyce aren't the only reason he's here."

"Folks we've got another lovely basket to sell," Matthew McKnight was calling out, thankfully sparing Claire from saying anything. "And it's not my fiancée's," Matthew continued. "Or I would be out in the audience bidding."

"Thanks for the heads up," someone called out from the gathered group. "When you stop auctioning and start bidding I'll know to give you some competition"

"Very funny, Anton," Matthew said with a nod toward the older man. "But you might end up eating with Cory after all."

"Your loss. My gain."

As the two chatted and badgered each other, Claire thought of Nik, Sheryl's words slipping through her mind. Then Mark Andrews picked up the next basket to be auctioned off, and her heart jumped.

"Mommy. That's yours," Emma whispered, leaning toward Claire.

"Shh. It's supposed to be a secret." Claire put her finger to her lips, then glanced behind her.

And looked directly into Nik's eyes. He, Cory and their mother were only ten feet away. Which made it likely he had heard Emma's stage whisper. Which made her think her daughter had said it on purpose.

She looked ahead, trying to still the erratic beating of her heart. This was crazy. She had to keep things under control.

The previous basket was now sold and then hers was being inspected by Matthew.

"So this one looks like a real winner. I wish I could bid on it myself," Matthew was saying. "I think I recognize some of the packaging." He glanced directly at Claire, winked at her, then held it up and the bidding started.

Claire desperately wanted to see who was bidding, but if Nik was, she didn't want to know. Mark was pointing to bidders, the amount of the bids increasing each time.

"Nik isn't bidding on your basket," Emma wailed, grabbing at her arm. "I should go over there and tell him to. I want to eat our basket with him."

Claire caught Emma's hand before she could make a move. She pulled her daughter onto her lap, wrapping her arms around her. "You just stay here, honey," Claire said. "We know just about everybody here, and whoever bids on my basket doesn't matter. The money is to fix up the kitchen in the church which is a good thing."

"But I want to sit with Nik," Emma complained, wiggling in Claire's arms.

"You just never mind," Claire said.

Claire forced her attention back to Matthew who was trying to keep up with the bids as they came in fast and furious. Claire was surprised herself at how high her basket was going but restrained her curiosity, keeping her attention on Matthew.

"300, 300, 325 anywhere, 300?" Matthew held his hand up glancing around, asking again. He waited for what seemed like forever then finally pointed in Claire's direction. "Sold," he called out. "To the newest member of our community, Nik Austen."

Emma spun around so fast she almost twisted Claire's hand. "Nik bought our basket," she crowed.

Claire's cheeks burned, as Nik walked up to Matthew and took the basket from him then walked over to Claire. "So I guess this means we get to eat together," he said. To her surprise he was smiling at her.

Suddenly his silence of the last few days, didn't matter as much.

"I'm not sure of the protocol," he said still holding her gaze. "What happens next?"

"My mom has a blanket, and we take it over to a spot under the trees and we put out the blanket and then we sit and eat our food," Emma said helpfully. She got up and to Claire's dismay, slipped her arm through Nik's. "We can go eat right now, we don't have to wait for the other baskets to sell."

Nik smiled down at Claire, and the fragile

hope his kiss had resurrected the other night became a gentle glow.

He switched the basket and held out his free hand to her. Her cheeks grew even redder as she tucked her folded blanket under one arm, took his hand and let him pull her up to her feet. She kept her head down as she walked alongside him holding her blanket in front of her like a shield. She knew her parents were there and most of the members of the church. This was a very public display of a very tentative relationship.

That Nik was willing to do what he did created a sense of expectation.

"This looks like a good spot," Emma announced when they came to a large tree. "Can you lay your blanket down, Mom? I'm getting really hungry."

Claire looked over her shoulder to where Cory and Joyce sat, dismayed to see Cory winking at her. "Did you want to sit with your mother and sister?" she asked Nik. From the way Cory was grinning at her, she would have preferred not to join her friend but it felt rude to ignore them.

"It's okay," Nik said. "I just arranged to visit them tomorrow for lunch. Besides, I bought your basket and that means I get to sit with you."

Claire shook up the blanket and let it settle, trying not to feel awkward, wishing she could dampen her expectation.

"My mom made some really good food," Emma said, kneeling down on the blanket. "She said we didn't have lots of good food in our kitchen, so I was allowed to help put the basket together. I took some of my favorite stuff from the cafe, and some healthy food, even though I think I like the other stuff better."

Her chatter filled the silence that had fallen between Nik and Claire.

"See, my mom put paper plates here and plastic utensils so we have something to eat with." Emma untied the ribbon at the top and pulled the cellophane off the basket, then looked up at Claire and Nik. "You guys can sit down, too."

Claire released a nervous laugh then did as Emma told her to. Nik sat on the other side of Emma.

"No. This is all wrong. You are supposed to sit together. Side by side," Emma commanded.

"I think Nik can sit where he wants," Claire said.

Emma seemed to realize she had overstepped but she didn't seem perturbed.

"But before we have to eat we need to pray."

"That's right," Claire agreed, giving her daughter a smile but also adding a warning look. Emma gave her an apologetic smile.

"So, let's pray," Claire said. And before she could fold her hands in her lap, Emma reached out to Nik and to Claire. She shot a sideways look at Nik, surprised to see him smiling at her, his hand outstretched.

She swallowed down her trepidation and took his hand. He curled his fingers around hers and once again her heart jumped. With a shake of her head, she turned her attention back to God, taking a moment to center herself. To know that she was approaching the Creator and Savior of the world.

She thanked God for the food and for the good weather and paused a moment before thanking him for the company and for the time they could spend together.

She said "Amen" just as Nik tightened his hand on hers. The warmth of his hand was a comfort and a connection she was loathe to break.

But Emma was handing out the plates and napkins, eager to begin.

"So, dig in," Claire said, handing Nik the basket.

"I'm sure it's all really good, but what is on the menu?"

"This one is a turkey, provolone and pesto sandwich, hopefully still warm," Claire said, taking out a foil and paper wrapped roll. "This one is Fontinie, prosciutto, fig and arugula on a ciabatta grilled on a panini maker. This one is Canadian bacon, sun dried tomato, spinach, soft mozzarella and secret sauce."

"Wow. These aren't just sandwiches. They sound like a gourmet feast." Nik scratched the side of his nose glancing at Emma. "Do you know what prosciutto is? Or pesto?"

Emma shrugged and shook her head. "Not really. I don't like them anyway." She dug into the basket and pulled out a package that had her name on it. "This one is for me," she said, showing it to Nik. "And it's my favorite."

"So, what's on that one?"

"Peanut butter and jelly."

Nik made a face. "Seriously? With all these amazing sounding sandwiches you're taking that?"

"It's the best."

"So, which one do you want?" Claire asked, turning the basket toward him.

"Why don't you pick for me?"

Claire handed him the turkey and pesto and took the Canadian bacon and tomato one for herself. She gave him a bottle of water and handed Emma a juice box.

They were quiet for a moment, concentrating on eating. In the background, Matthew was still calling out bids, encouraging people to go higher. People were laughing and above and around them a faint breeze whispered through the trees.

Emma was done eating in mere seconds. She slurped her juice down then, to Claire's surprise, brushed the crumbs off her clothes and jumped to her feet. "Marla and Chris are playing on the slides. Can I go?"

"Sure. I guess." Claire had thought for sure she would want to stay with Nik, especially after her little stunt the other night when she finagled a Chinese checkers game out of him.

Emma was off like a shot, her hair streaming behind her.

"She's a busy one, isn't she?" Nik said, watching her running to the park.

"Tell me," Claire said.

"It must be difficult, managing her and your business, and keeping sane at the same time."

"How do you know I'm sane?" Claire said with

a grin, surprised once again at how comfortable she felt with him.

"I don't think you're insane," Nik protested, looking taken aback.

"Do you think I'm incapable? Or incompetent or ingenious?"

"I think you're capable, competent and probably a genius."

"Flatterer," she said, her heart opening up at their easy ribbing. In spite of what had happened the other night, or maybe because of it, she felt surprisingly comfortable around him.

She took another bite of her sandwich just as some sauce dribbled down her chin. She swiped at it, her cheeks flushing.

Then to her dismay, Nik smiled, took her chin in his hand and dabbed the corner of her mouth. "There. Now you're all good."

But he didn't let go of her chin and his eyes locked on hers. She swallowed, her breath quickening, her heart fluttering.

Then his fingers lightly caressed her cheek and he dropped his hand.

"About the other night..." he started.

But she waved off his apology.

"It's okay. I understand." She didn't want to hear his regrets about kissing her. He was too close, and she was feeling too vulnerable. He had turned her world upside down and she still wasn't sure what to think of it all. She had her daughter to consider, yet the loneliness haunting her the past few years, the desire to have someone think about her, think about her needs, had only grown.

"I wanted you to know I wasn't apologizing for kissing you," he continued despite her protest. "I was trying to say I was sorry for breaking down on you. I have to confess I didn't feel very manly."

Her heart shifted, and she felt a sudden relief.

"I think it takes a real man to express his emotions. To be vulnerable." She gave him a careful smile, surprised at how good his confession made her feel.

"Maybe, but it's not manly to admit to."

"Probably not, but I'm glad you trusted me enough to let me know. It's seldom men are so willing to open up."

Nik tilted his head to one side as if examining her from another angle. "You sound sad. Are you thinking about Emma's father?"

"You're way too astute for me," she said.

"What was he like?"

"It doesn't matter," she said giving her head a shake.

"I wish I could say it didn't, but given that I kissed you and wasn't sorry I did, given that I broke down in your arms and that, in front of your entire community, I bought your lunch basket, I think it matters a little."

His words created a tiny thrill, a beat of expectation, a glimmer of hope.

"Tell me," he insisted.

She shrugged and gave in.

"Andy Donnel was the first real boyfriend I ever had. We dated in high school, and I was crazy about him, but he wasn't very demonstrative, and I accepted that because I didn't know any different. Looking back now, I think we slipped from being friends to dating, to getting engaged. It was easy and convenient. We'd known each other all our lives. It wasn't the great romantic love story, but I thought that's just how things went. After we were engaged, he put pressure on me to... to be more... intimate..." her voice faded off as she looked down, struggling with the usual shame she knew she shouldn't carry but couldn't let go of.

"It's okay, I think I know where you're going," Nik said. "You don't have to say anything more."

"Anyway, we pushed the wedding date up, got married, moved into a tiny apartment and after Emma was born Andy changed."

"How so?" Nik encouraged.

Part of her wanted to stop but everyone around her knew her story so she had never talked about Andy and the repercussions for her. What it had truly been like.

"He would go to the bar after work, come home drunk and angry, accusing me and Emma of ruining his life." Claire shook her head, glancing over to where Emma was playing, laughing and running around. "As if that beautiful child was something to regret."

"She certainly isn't."

He sounded sad and Claire shot him a puzzled look, but he was looking at Emma as well, his eyes holding the same sorrow his voice did. She sensed his story held more layers, but then he seemed to shake it off.

"So, what happened to him?" he continued. "Did he leave you?"

"Yes. He did." It had been over five years but the betrayal still stung. "I remember waking up the next morning and he wasn't there. At first, I thought he might be sleeping off another bender. I brought Emma to the day home. But when I came home from work, Andy still wasn't back." Claire stopped a moment, fighting down the usual anger her memories created. The humiliation. She took a deep, calming breath and carried on. "A couple of days later I got a text from him. He wasn't coming home. He didn't want to have anything to do with me or Emma. He wanted a divorce." She didn't add the other awful things he had said. Though she deleted the text as soon as she read it, the words were indelibly branded into her mind.

"I'm sorry to hear that," Nik said, taking her hand in his again.

"I was, too." She kept her eyes on their interlocked hands, her thumb caressing the back of his. It felt good to hold his hand, larger than her own, holding a few scars, large and strong.

"So you're divorced?"

"Actually, no. We never did manage to get the papers signed. I'm a widow. Andy was killed crossing the street as he left a bar a year ago. He still had life insurance and I was still the beneficiary which gave me something at least."

"But not enough for a down payment on the house?"

"I used the money to start Coffee Creek. I figured I needed income before I could buy a house.

I kept a few thousand aside for my house fund. Selling Andy's car was supposed to top it up." She shook her head. "But we both know how that ended."

"You've had a hard road, too," he said.

She gave him a sad-half-smile as acknowledgement. "I have. But I was blessed to have the support of my family and my church community."

"No condemnation from them?"

"Of course not. I'm sure there were a few people who thought I should have done more. Andy's mother being one of them."

"Are Andy's parents still around here?"

"No. Andy's father died before we got married so at least he didn't have to see what happened to his son. His mother moved to Florida."

"Does she ever seem Emma?"

Another flicker of pain. "No. She was always convinced Emma wasn't Andy's child. And she was never close to Andy. So she has stayed out of our lives."

Nik sighed lightly. "That must hurt."

"It did at one time. But I can't change her mind and, truthfully, it's a little easier this way. My parents love Emma to death and she has no memory of her father or my in-laws. So I'm hoping I've done right by her. It's tough being a single mom. You're always second guessing every choice you make."

"I'm sure it is," Nik said, pausing before asking his next question. "Do you ever feel like you can't do it anymore? Be a mom?"

"There are times where I've wondered if I should have married Andy. Wondered if maybe Emma wouldn't have been better off if I had given her up. But I was never alone in all of this. Like I said, I had my family and I had my faith. My prayers and the prayers of my family held me up. If I had been on my own, who knows what choices I might have made."

"Choices like my mother made." Nik pulled his hands out of hers and leaned against the tree behind him, looking over to where his mother, Cory and now Matthew were sitting.

"Are you still struggling with that?"

Nik kept his eyes averted and Claire wondered if she were pushing too hard. But she knew things were shifting between them. They were moving in a dangerous direction. She couldn't simply go with the flow and see where it took her. She had Emma to think of.

And she had her own heart to watch.

So, she had to know where he was at with his other relationships.

"It's hard sometimes. I've held onto my anger against my mother so long, I'm not sure how to dump it or where."

"What would your foster mother say?" she asked, sensing this woman had a large influence on his life.

Nik chuckled lightheartedly, then turned back to Claire. She was happy to see a genuine smile on his face. "She would say I should put it at the foot of the cross."

"That sounds like a good place to put a lot of what burdens us."

"Is it that easy though?"

Claire thought of her anger with Andy. Her pain at his desertion of her and his rejection of their daughter. Her own struggles, even now, with the house and what she wanted.

"It should be, though I don't do it as often as I should, either."

"Well, as far as my mother goes, my friend gave me some good advice. He said sometimes, if one goes through the motions, the feelings will follow. So I will make work of being with my mother and sister. Spend more time with them."

Claire swallowed at the sincerity in his voice. At what he was suggesting.

If he was spending more time with them, would he become more connected to this place?

Would he change his mind about staying?

CHAPTER 9

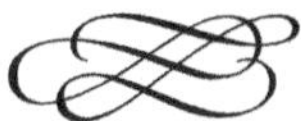

Nik turned off his truck but stayed inside, looking at the church.

The last time he'd been inside a church was at Rebecca's funeral. He'd felt the heavy burden of guilt over not spending enough time with his foster mother, grief at her loss and anger with God for taking such a godly woman too soon.

He'd paid little attention to the minister and when the funeral was over, he stayed long enough to pass his condolences to Rebecca's two children before he fled.

He hadn't entered a church building since. He figured if he left God alone, God, too, would leave him be.

However, in the past few days, God seemed to

have broken into his life. Coming up more often in conversation. Making His presence known.

So, that morning Nik decided that maybe he should go to church. Maybe he should figure out why things had come together in his life the way they had.

Was it a coincidence that his mother had moved to the very town Nik needed to leave?

Coincidence that the woman who invaded his thoughts and dreams currently lived in the house he hoped to tear down? The house she saw as a dream come true for her and her daughter?

He didn't like that his plans had become amorphous.

Had God really brought him to this place as Chance insinuated?

"Enough," he told himself as he stepped out of the truck and into the warm fall air. The sun shone benevolently and music streamed through the windows of the church as he strode up the sidewalk.

A perfect Sunday, he thought, stepping into the foyer.

To one side was the entrance to the sanctuary; to the other a large open area where a few people congregated, drank coffee and talked. He glanced around but he saw neither Claire nor his mother nor Cory. He hadn't seen Claire leave but her car was gone so he assumed she was here.

"Nik. You *are* here!"

A sticky hand grabbed his own, and when he turned around, there was Emma, her grin as big as the huge pink sequined bow clipped in her hair. "My mom is talking, talking and talking to Aunty Tess and it's getting bo-o-o-ring." She rolled her eyes for added emphasis.

"Well, we don't want that, now, do we?" Nik said, surprised at the surge of joy that seeing her gave him.

"Let's go find her. I want her to know you're here. She was talking about you to Aunty Tess."

"Really? What was she saying?"

Emma gave an exaggerated shrug. "I don't know. Mommy told me to get a cookie."

"Look who I found," Emma announced, dragging Nik to Claire and Tess, both of whom were partially hidden by large plants. Claire wore a skirt that skimmed her knees, flat black shoes and a soft blue shirt with long sleeves. Her hair was loose, waving over her shoulders, shining in the overhead lights. She looked stunning.

Claire's cheeks flushed when she glanced at him and their eyes met. Then Tess, who was closest to him, held out her hand.

"Welcome to our service," she said, shaking his hand. "Glad you could be here."

"Me too." He gave Tess a brief smile, before he returned his attention to Claire. "I was thinking about what you said yesterday, at the picnic, and decided I would come this morning."

"Well, I'm glad you came," she said. Her eyes flitted to Emma. "Sounds like church is starting. Honey, you should go wash your hands."

The music from the sanctuary behind them swelled and people trickled out of the open area they stood in.

"Are you here with your mother and sister?" Tess asked as Emma flounced off.

"No. I came on my own. Are they here yet?"

"I haven't seen them," Tess replied. She looked at him, her eyes narrowed, as if assessing him.

What did Claire say to her? He couldn't help but wonder.

"Anyhow, I should get going," she continued. Tess gave Claire a quick hug then left.

"Everything okay?" Nik asked.

"Yeah. It's all good." Claire's voice was a bit shaky, which increased his curiosity. But he didn't have the nerve to question her further. "I should go find Emma and sit down," she said. She hesitated, then turned to him. "Are you waiting for your mother or… or do you want to sit with Emma and me?"

He held her gaze, wondering if this was some test.

"I'd love to sit with you and Emma. Thank you." He felt like he should wait for his mother and sister, but Claire was right there and after yesterday he wanted to spend more time with her, not less.

He'd meet Joyce and Cory for lunch after church, anyway.

Claire's smile reinforced that he'd made the right choice.

When Emma returned she was delighted to see Nik still standing with her mother. And when Claire took her hand, and walked toward the sanctuary, Emma grabbed his. Claire shot him a worried glance, but he responded with a smile. They looked like a little family walking into church together and despite his plans, despite the things he wanted to do, it felt right. As if the gap cloven into his life with the loss of his child was now filled.

They found an empty spot toward the back of the church, thankfully. While Nik was glad to be sitting with Claire and Emma, he also knew the possible social repercussions for her. Bad enough that yesterday they had spent most of the afternoon together; sitting with her in church so soon afterward seems to create another declaration.

Besides, Nik wasn't ready to face Claire's mother again. Yesterday she had come by while he and Claire were talking and he could tell from her scowl she wasn't happy with the situation.

"Do you like my new hair bow?" Emma asked, patting her head proudly. "My grandma bought it for me for my birthday. I wanted the purple one, but the pink one was the only one they had left she said. All my friends have one. Marla has four. I'd really like to have four, but my mommy says I'm paying more for the name on the tag than I am for the bow. Except I don't know what that means. How can you pay for a tag?"

Nik shot a glance at Claire who shook her head in dismay. "Honey, I don't think Mr. Nik wants to hear about your hair bow in church." She tucked Emma's hair behind her ear. "But I'm glad you like it. Even though it isn't purple." Claire pulled out a piece of paper from her purse. "Now, why don't you work on the children's bulletin so you can change your attention to why we're here."

Emma took the paper and the pencil her mother offered her. "I know. I shouldn't have been so proud of my bow. God doesn't care what we look like on the outside, He cares what we look like on the inside," she said primly.

Despite the truth of what Emma said, Nik checked a smile. Once again, he glanced at Claire and caught the twinkle in her eye.

And at that moment all was well with his soul.

The church service began with lively singing that reminded him of the church his foster mother attended.

He recognized a couple of the songs and sang along, surprised at how easily the words and tune came back to him.

When the singing ended, the pastor came to the front of the church and looked around with a smile. He didn't seem a lot older than Nik himself, but when he spoke his voice had an air of authority and wisdom.

"Let's turn in our Bibles to Isaiah 49." He paused and the only sound in the church was the fluttering of pages, an occasional cough. A holy hush alighted in that moment.

"Shout for joy, you heavens; rejoice, you earth; burst into song, you mountains!" As he read, Nik thought of the mountains cradling this valley that he so admired. The mountains. "For the Lord comforts his people and will have compassion on his afflicted ones." Again, Nik's mind went back to the pain he suffered here and regardless of his doubts about God's care, a tendril of love slivered through his soul.

"Can a mother forget the baby at her breast and have no compassion on the child she has borne? Though she may forget, I will not forget you. See I have engraved you on the palms of my hands."

Nik's heartbeat gathered speed with each word the Pastor read. Chance had spoken the same words to him. And they resonated with him now.

He always thought his mother had forgotten him. But had she?

Her tears had shown him otherwise.

He cast a sidelong glance at Claire. Her focus was on the minister, but her hand rested on Emma's head, her fingers absently twining in her daughter's hair.

A mother who loved her daughter and would do anything for her.

A woman whom he admired and who was growing increasingly important to him. She must have sensed him looking at her because she turned her head, her eyes meeting his. In that moment awareness arced between them and from her quick intake of breath he sensed she felt it too.

He swallowed, then before he could stop himself, he rested his hand on her shoulder, connecting them with this tenuous touch.

Her smile was like a benediction and it settled deep in his soul.

* * *

"NIK IS BACK," Emma yelled from the kitchen.

Ever since Claire and Emma had come back from church, Emma had parked herself in the bay window waiting for Nik to return from visiting his mother, his sister and Matthew.

"I'm going to go see him," Emma called out again.

"Maybe wait a bit, honey," Claire returned, setting her book aside and getting up from the chair she'd curled up in. They had just come back from a very noisy visit with her parents, aunt and uncle and cousins and she was thankful for the quiet and a chance to read. "He probably has things he needs to do."

"But it's Sunday," Emma said, already standing by the door when Claire came into the kitchen. "He's not supposed to work today."

"Not everybody feels that way," Claire said. "Besides some people need to work on Sunday. Like doctors and nurses."

Emma fidgeted, looking poised to leave.

Claire wanted to let her go, but she was still sorting out her feelings about Nik. Sitting beside him in church, watching him listen so intently to the minister and even singing along with some of the songs had shifted her last resistance to him. She knew his foster mother had taught him about God and faith and she could tell this morning that being in church was not new to him. That it meant something.

Nik was moving her closer to a point of no return. She still had a chance to turn back, to keep her heart whole.

But every time she was with him, their connection grew deeper.

Part of her was tired of fighting her feelings for him. She wanted to give in and forget that he had plans to destroy the very house that meant so much to her. Forget that after he was done with that, he would leave again. Forget that the trailer in the yard represented his temporary presence in her world.

Emma looked out the window of the door and squealed. "He's coming over here, and he's got a baseball glove and a ball. He said he would teach me how to catch better."

And before Claire could stop her, Emma was out the door and clattering down the wooden steps, running toward Nik.

Claire stepped out as well, hugging her waist as Emma danced around Nik, Mooch joining them, barking his pleasure.

"I hope you don't mind, but I thought maybe we could play catch," he said to Claire.

"That's absolutely fine," Claire said, joy trickling through her.

"You should play too, Mommy," Emma called out, her grin almost splitting her face.

"Why don't you go get your baseball glove," Claire said to her, "and we can practice altogether."

"Yay," Emma cried out. She charged across the yard and into the house, the door banging shut behind her.

"Did you have a good lunch with your mother and Cory?" Claire asked in the silence that followed Emma's departure.

"I think I'm getting the hang of this being a brother and a son."

"I think you'll be good at it," Claire said.

"I hope so, too," Nik said his eyes steady.

Another silence fell and a soft question floated into Claire's mind.

Could he get the hang of being a husband and father?

The question rose, and finally settled.

His gaze wore at her thin veneer of resistance. When he cupped her face in his rough hand, his fingers caressing her cheek, her pulse spiked.

She wondered for a moment if he would kiss her. He took a step forward, leaning closer. Her breath disappeared as expectation and anticipation swelled between them.

Then the door of the house flew open and Emma was back, her energy and enthusiasm shattering the moment.

Nik jumped back, and Claire looked away. Like a bunch of teenagers caught by their parents.

She glanced over at Nik surprised to see him smiling. Was he thinking the same thing?

"I found my glove, now we can play?" Emma called out. "Mom, you go stand by the house, Nik, you go to the fence and I'll stand by the flower bed."

Nik saluted, and they each took their respective places, Mooch bounding from one to the other.

"Mooch. Sit."

Claire and Nik spoke at exactly the same time then laughed as Mooch did what they'd told him.

"See? Mooch listens really good," Emma said.

They lobbed the ball back and forth, Nik coaching Emma on how to hold her glove and how to throw. Slowly she got the hang of it. Mooch stayed where he was, clearly intimidated by the command from both Nik and Claire. But he whined as his head followed the ball.

"I think Mooch really wants to play," Emma said, patting him on the head.

The dog took that as permission to get up and when Claire threw the ball to Emma, Mooch jumped into the air, caught it in his mouth and took off.

"Mooch, come back," Emma called out.

"Get back here, you silly dog," Nik yelled at the same time.

They took off after the dog, but he swerved, easily avoiding them. Nik cornered him by his trailer but Mooch ran around the back and came out between it and the flower bed and headed directly toward Claire, with Nik and Emma in pursuit. Mooch ran into Claire just as Nik tackled him. Emma ran into Nik, putting him off balance and everyone ended up in a jumbled heap on the grass.

Mooch squirmed away, leaving Emma on top of Claire, whose arm was pinned under Nik.

Claire laughed and was soon joined by Emma and Nik. Then Mooch, as if sensing he was missing something, returned, licking all their faces which made them laugh harder.

Finally, Nik rose, resting on one elbow, gently moving Claire's arm out from under him. "I'm so sorry," he said, his grin fading, but staying where he was, his head silhouetted against the blue, blue sky. "Are you okay?"

"I'm fine," she said still chuckling, holding his eyes, her heartbeat ticking upward.

"I'm okay, too," Emma put in, scooching up, sitting cross-legged on the grass.

"I'm glad to hear that," Nik said, his eyes flicking to hers but returning to Claire's.

She felt pinned to the ground. As if his eyes held her there. She didn't want to move or look away.

The moment grew and expanded, obliterating everything around them. Creating a bubble holding only them.

"Are you going to kiss my mommy again?" Emma teased.

The bubble burst.

"Again?" Claire asked, struggling to sit up, the

magic doused by the reality of what Emma had just said. "What are you talking about?" She fought to keep her tone light, as if Emma might have been mistaken.

"I saw you. You and Nik. Kissing in the living room." Emma pressed her hands to her chest in a dramatic gesture. "That made me so, so happy."

Claire shot a glance Nik's way to gauge his reaction and, to her surprise, he was smiling.

He stood then extended a hand to Claire. She shot him a warning look but took his hand. Once she was upright, he didn't let go. Instead, he gave her hand a little, teasing tug.

"I think we could give Emma what she wants," he said, his tone low, intimate.

The smoldering in his eyes made her breath hitch in her throat. She swallowed, about to make a feeble protest but then his head obliterated the sky and his lips touched hers. It was the briefest of contacts. Hardly even a kiss. But her mouth burned and her heart raced in her chest.

And then, before she could stop herself, she leaned in and kissed him back. His mouth was soft, warm and his arm came around her waist, pulling her close to him. For the space of a heartbeat they clung to each other.

Then he pulled away, plucking a couple of

blades of grass out of her hair, tossing them aside. “There. Now you’re all better.”

She couldn’t believe how casual he was. How easily he’d given in to Emma’s request. And how unselfconscious he was. He looked as if kissing her in front of her daughter was the most natural thing in the world.

She struggled with the implications of it all but as she held his gaze the hope smoldering in Claire’s heart grew.

CHAPTER 10

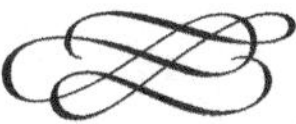

Nik brushed the grass off his clothes, his eyes locked on Claire. Hundreds of thoughts chased themselves though his mind but one clear thought was uppermost.

He had kissed Claire in front of her daughter.

And he didn't regret it at all.

"So, are we still playing?" Emma called out. "I got the ball."

Nik dragged his gaze from Claire and looked over to Emma. Sure enough she held the baseball between two fingers, pulling a face of disgust. "It's kind of wet though."

"Then maybe we should let it dry out," Nik said. Holding a ball full of dog slobber held no appeal.

"You okay?" he asked, looking back at Claire, pleased to see her smiling.

"Yeah. Fine."

"Really? Cause I am. I truly am. Just in case you were wondering." He hoped she understood what he was trying to say. Maybe he was jumping ahead but the past few days had changed so much. Being with Claire and Emma at the picnic had felt so right. As had sitting with them in church.

And this afternoon, visiting with his mother and sister and future brother-in-law had given him a glimpse of the other possibilities that lay here in Sweet Creek.

He wasn't sure if Claire felt the same about him as he did about her.

Would she have kissed you back if she didn't?

But even as these thoughts slipped through his mind he looked at the house behind her and a shadow slid over the day.

"Where are you?" Claire asked. She must have seen how his expression changed. "Reliving memories?"

"Yeah. Sorry." He shook his head as if trying to dislodge them.

Then, to his surprise, Claire lifted her hand

and stroked his cheek. "I pray that someday they will ease."

At her touch, he felt as if that was happening already.

"I hope so too," Nik said. "Though visiting with my mother helped."

"Are you finding your way through to forgiving her?"

Nik tested that idea a moment, looking past Claire to Emma, who had given up on them and was now throwing the ball for Mooch to fetch.

"I had an interesting conversation with her," he said, resting his hands on his hips, pulling in a long breath. "She wanted to know about my life after I was moved out of the Jensen's home. It was a tough moment."

"Did you tell her?"

"I wanted to. I thought of all that had happened here but then..." his voice drifted as he looked back at the house, walking toward it. He rested his hand against the post supporting the roof over the porch, running his fingers over the rough wood. It was still there.

"You look like you're remembering something," Claire said, sitting on the steps of the porch.

"I remember this dent here," he said, running

his finger back and forth over it. "My foster father was angry with me because I mouthed him off. He grabbed a flipper from the barbecue and came at me. I ducked, he missed, hit this post and I took off. I laid low for the rest of the day, wandering around town hoping he was gone or passed out when I got back."

"I'm so sorry."

He sat down beside her, watching Emma wrestle with Mooch.

"Being with my mother made me realize telling her wouldn't change anything," he said, his voice quiet. "Something the pastor said this morning stuck with me. How a mother's love can take different forms. How it's not always about hugs and kisses. How love can be about making hard choices." He released another sigh, remembering the sorrow on his mother's face. The glisten of tears in her eyes. Again. "I actually felt sorry for her this afternoon."

"That's a good place to start."

"I know. It's like each time I see her, listen to her, spend time with her, I come around to another place in my journey with her. It's like a spiral that gets tighter and tighter and with each revolution, I get a little closer to her and a little further from my emotions. It took a few years to get to this point but for the first time in a long time I realized that it wasn't her fault I ended up here. In this house. With that family."

Claire's eyes locked onto his and she gave him a tender smile. "That's a journey that was worth taking."

"I know. I'm so glad I came here." And he returned her smile, his soul filled by just sitting beside this amazing woman. "And I'm thankful I met you. And Emma."

"Me too." Her response warmed his heart.

She looked past him her expression shifting, a faint frown creasing her forehead.

"What are you thinking about?" he asked.

"My own remembrances of this place." She leaned back against the other post, pulling her knees up close and hugging them with her arms.

"Which ones are you pulling out?"

She shook her head, giving him a melancholy smile. "Doesn't matter. I don't want to trivialize what you just told me."

"I was only sharing my particular memory. You have your own that are as legitimate as mine. So tell me."

She smiled, her eyes growing bright as if slipping back to another time. "I remember Tess and me climbing up on this porch roof with a blanket, a bottle of water and a bag of cookies we had filched from the kitchen."

"So you're telling me I'm sitting with a thief?" Nik teased, wanting to lighten the mood that had clung to him.

"The worst kind. The kind that steals from her own mother." Claire's smile grew as she settled back. "We would do that often. Sometimes we would pretend we were princesses stuck in a tower, waiting for our prince to rescue us until it got too hot and then we would decamp and slither down that post behind you. We always pleaded with our parents to let us sleep on the roof. For some reason they always said no." She chuckled at the memory and he joined in.

"Those are good things to remember."

"And they are part of this house too," she said, looking away from him, as if unwilling to see his reaction.

"I suppose," he said. "I wish I could have experienced some of that."

As soon as he spoke he wished he could take the words back. He sounded as if he were feeling sorry for himself.

"I also wish this house had better memories for you."

Nik looked back, struggling yet with his

mixed emotions. "I do too." It was all he could tell her.

And yet his mind ticked back to kissing her in the living room. An event which, they had just discovered, Emma had witnessed.

He looked over at Claire again, their eyes meeting. Four feet separated them, but the connection was so strong it felt like inches.

Stay.

The single word eased like a sigh into his confused mind, settling feather-light yet carrying a weight of peace.

Stay.

Again, he looked back at Claire, a woman who had her own struggles and demons to wrestle. Who'd come out strong and in charge of her life. A mother who took care of her child. Who would do anything for her. Someone who not only knew what the words "Mother" and "Faithful" were, but who lived them.

Stay.

Could he?

Did he seriously think he could leave feeling the way he did about Claire? About Emma?

* * *

"YOU'RE HUMMING." Tess looked up from the industrial dishwasher as she loaded the last of the dishes, grinning at Claire. "It's been a long, busy day, and you're still humming.

"Am I humming?" Claire adjusted her bandanna, wrung out a cloth and wiped down the countertop.

"Loudly and cheerfully," Tess said as she closed the large metal door. "Too cheerfully for someone who is working, I might add. Does this have anything to do with spending all day Sunday with Nik?"

"Not the whole day." Claire couldn't stop the faint flush warming her neck and turned away so Tess couldn't catch it and start her standard cross-examination of Claire post-date.

She wasn't sure she was ready to talk more about him to Tess. Her feelings for Nik were deepening. With each kiss he gave her hope grew. "Did he give you lots of smooches?" Tess asked, hitting the button.

"I don't smooch and tell," Claire said, too late realizing how prim she sounded.

"Since when?" Tess scoffed, turning back to her sister. "I always got to hear the low down on kissability and scoring of said kissability."

"Well, I'm not about to score Nik." Claire

stirred up the dough, her movements quick and decisive.

"So, you did kiss him."

Caught.

"And?" Tess wouldn't leave it alone.

"It was nice." Claire continued wiping. "And that's all I'm telling you."

"Was Emma there?" Tess' voice grew serious and Claire glanced across the kitchen to catch her sister's now-somber gaze.

"Yes. She was. And I don't need the lecture about being responsible with my daughter. I know what's at stake. So does Nik."

"I know you do. So I'm thinking things must be getting serious."

Claire blinked as she stared down at the cloth. "They are."

"You sound confused."

"I am. A little. He's a wonderful guy and he cares about Emma and he likes me. He even puts up with Mooch."

"All in his favor. I don't even like that mutt."

Claire wasn't sure if she dared venture down the next part, but Nik's comment allowed a glimmer of hope to grow within her. "And as far as the house goes, I think he's coming around."

"Why is that so important to you? It's just a house."

"You know it's more than just a house," Claire said. "I've always seen it as a way to take care of Emma. As a way of connecting with my past."

"Could it be that you're making too much of that house, too?" Tess asked.

"Maybe, but it would mean so much if he would understand what that house means to me."

"I understand, but you could switch that around too," Tess said, sounding imminently reasonable.

Claire held that thought a moment then shook her head as all Nik's motivations and reasons for his actions tumbled back. "He has a deeper, darker reason for tearing that house down. Some horrible things happened to him there. Abuse, neglect at the hands of the foster parents he had then. He thinks if he gets rid of the house those memories and pain will go away and that concerns me."

"Why?"

"To me it shows how deeply he's still stuck in the past. And if he can't get over that, what kind of relationship could we have?"

Tess nodded, as if understanding what her sister was saying.

Claire took a breath, winding the still-damp cloth around her hands. "Besides, he's not building another house there. He wants to put up a fourplex."

The look of shock on Tessa's face gave Claire more ammunition for her reactions to Nik's plan.

"That would be criminal," Tess said.

"I agree. It's a gorgeous property, and I know the yard is huge, but if he built the fourplex there, it would take over the whole yard. So that was one of the other reasons I wasn't happy what he wants to do."

Tess tapped finger on her lower lip. "So you think he still might do that?"

Claire shook her head. "I hope not. He knows how much that house means to me and Emma. And if… if things change enough between us, I had hoped…" she let the sentence trail off, unwilling to vocalize the wish that glowed deep in her soul.

"Hoped that the three of you could live there," Tess said, finishing the thought.

Claire wasn't sure she dared voice her dreams yet.

"And what about his relationship with his mother? Has he made peace with her yet?" Tess asked.

"He visited her yesterday after church, and he seemed happy when he came back." Claire rinsed the cloth and wrung it out once more then tossed it into the laundry bin. "I think things are moving in the right direction between him and Joyce."

"So, things seem to be falling into place for you as well?"

Claire untied her apron and tossed it into the laundry bin. "I feel like they are, and yet there's a part of me that is still afraid."

"I don't blame you. It's hard to trust when trust has been broken. Even if the person you care for wasn't the one who caused that to happen."

Claire's expression grew serious as she looked at her sister. "And you and Jace are okay?"

Tess looked down at the sparkling ring on her finger and released a gentle smile. "We are more than okay. And I'm not worried about the future. Jace is a good man and I know he will take care of me."

"You two have been through a lot, too," Claire said. "Getting past what Carson MacGregor did to you can't be easy. Especially because he was Jace's boss at one time."

Tess tapped her fingers on the counter, frowning. "It hasn't been easy but I feel like I should let you know, Jace told me last night that two other women are filing sexual assault charges against Carson. I… I asked if I should join the suit. Jason said it was my call. I'm not sure I want to dredge up all that stuff again. I feel like I plowed through that dark valley and came up the other side stronger. To be a part of this suit might drag me back there. But I don't think I should leave those girls on their own."

Claire came around the counter and pulled her sister into her arms, hugging her tight. "I want you to know that no matter what happens, we're all behind you. We're all supporting you and we're all praying for you."

Tess hugged her back, clinging to her a moment. "I am so thankful for you. We're so blessed to have each other."

"Nik said the same thing. He said he was always jealous of our relationship."

"I guess he knows a good thing when he sees it." Tess released a shaky laugh.

Claire gave Tess one final hug then drew back.

"We've talked enough about me the past few months," Tess said. "What do you think will happen with you and Nik?"

For a moment uncertainty gripped Claire, but behind that came the memory of his kiss. The talks they had. "I think Nik knows what's at stake if we get more serious. He's been on the receiving end of brokenness in families and I also sense he's searching for security as well."

"I feel like I should tell you, I gave him the sister talk."

"What?" Claire shot her sister a puzzled look.

"You know. The one where I tell him he has to be careful with Emma and with you and that if he hurts you I will hunt him down like an animal and punch him in the face."

"You didn't."

Tess lifted her hands in a 'what can I do' gesture. "Okay, I didn't say I would punch him in the face. That was just embellishment to let you know I was serious. But I told him to be careful. So I'm thinking if he's still with you and he's still kissing you he's not being casual about this relationship."

Claire felt the same way but hearing her sister say it made her situation more real.

"I was going to ask if you wanted to help me pick out table decorations for the wedding, but I imagine you'll be seeing him tonight?" Tess asked.

"No. He's gone for a couple of days. He told me he wouldn't be back until Wednesday. He had to do some follow up on a potential job—"

"Where?"

"He didn't say where. But the fact that he's looking into other work is good. Originally, he said after he was done with the house, he would be gone on a six-month vacation. He hasn't said anything more about that." Claire clung to the vague plans she was weaving around Nik's vague plans, hoping, once again, that he wanted to settle down.

In Sweet Creek.

"But tonight doesn't work, anyway," Claire continued. "I promised Emma a mother/daughter night. She wants to do pedicures. She said she wants to look nice for when Nik comes back."

"She seems attached to him."

Claire thought of them playing ball the day before and smiled. "She's been campaigning for him from the start. Going on about not having a daddy and how she thought Nik would make a good one. So she's good with how things are progressing."

"Are you a little concerned about her attachment?"

"I was. But you know, I feel good about it all. Things are changing between Nik and me. I could hold back, but for how long? I need to take a chance once in a while." Claire bumped her sister with her hip. "Just like you've told me to."

"Sounds like things are coming together for you, my dear," Tess said as they walked out of the back of the cafe.

"I think so." Claire knew she had to be wary yet she was tired of it. She had to trust as well that the prayers she had been sending up the past few weeks were being heard.

She had to keep praying and trust that God would give her and Emma the strength to deal with whatever came their way. She hoped she wouldn't have to pray *that* prayer too soon.

They said goodbye and Claire got in her car. Her phone had been dead all day so she plugged it in. As soon as she started the car it pinged. But the screen was still black. It would take a minute or two before the phone had enough charge for her to check her messages. As she drove it pinged again, but she figured she would check it when she got to her mother's place.

But once she arrived, her mother was standing by her car with Emma and Mooch who had his leash clipped to his collar. Clearly everyone was ready to go. Immediately.

"Everything okay?" Claire asked, catching her mother's faint frown.

"Emma, can you and Mooch wait in the car a moment?" her mother asked.

They helped Emma and the dog inside then her mother caught Claire by the arm and drew her a ways down the driveway.

"I had hoped we could sit down and have a little chat in the house," her mother said as they walked, then stopped around the corner of the garage. "But I couldn't get out of this appointment and my company will be back any minute."

"What did you want to chat about?" The second the question left her mouth Claire regretted asking. She could see by the way her mother's lips thinned that it would not be a pleasant conversation.

Her mother turned to her, concern etched into her features. "I saw you and Nik in church on Sunday. With Emma."

"So?" The question came out snippier than she'd intended. She blamed it on a mixture of her changing feelings for Nik and a touch of insecurity about her decision.

"And he bought your basket at the picnic."

"All of this I know," Claire said, folding her arms. Claire knew exactly where her mother was headed.

"I'm worried about you and Emma. All she

could do was talk about him and how she was so hoping he would be her daddy. I tried to temper her enthusiasm, but she seemed to think this was a done deal. Has he proposed to you without talking to us?"

This, Claire could handle. "No, Mother. He hasn't proposed. Emma is just making mountains out of molehills. Though I have to confess, I've never seen a molehill, so I wouldn't know how one could do that."

Her mother snorted in annoyance. "You and Tess are the same." She pulled in her breath, smoothing a hand over her hair. "But I am concerned. I understand he is tearing the house down and building an apartment block."

Claire wished she could firmly tell her mother it wasn't her business but she also knew her mother was truly worried.

"How do you know?" she asked, going for deflection instead.

Her mother heaved out a sigh. "I overheard Gerald saying that he finagled the clawfoot bathtub in the house from Nik before he demolishes it."

"And here I thought you would discuss the sermon, not plumbing possibilities," she joked stifling her concerns. She had thought Nik was having second thoughts.

Her mother waved her joke off. "At any rate, I don't think he has intentions of staying around."

"How do you figure that?"

"That he's leaving?" Her mother bit her lip and took a moment to reply. "Apparently, Nik was also asking Gerald about a recent trip he made overseas and if he had any suggestions for a trip he wanted to make."

"How long were you listening to this conversation?" Claire tried to inject some humor into her voice, but her mother's comments disturbed her. "And where was I?"

Her mother had the grace to look a little discomfited as she lifted one shoulder in a shrug. "I just happened to be behind them as we walked out of church. It took a while. And I don't know where you were. Probably busy talking to your friends."

Claire's mind skipped back, drawing out a memory of Kelsey Swain pulling her aside to talk about baseball practice. She remembered wondering how Nik would do but then she saw him talking to Walt the plumber.

"I don't have much time to say much more," her mother continued. "But I feel I need to warn you about Nik. Warn you not to make the same mistake you made with Lance."

Claire sucked in a deep breath, struggling to calm a surge of frustrated anger. "I think I learned my lesson from that situation," she snapped.

Her mother frowned but then looked over at Emma, who was sitting quietly in the car. "You should probably go. But realize that this time around you're not just deciding for yourself. You have Emma to consider. If this man is doing what I keep hearing he's doing — tearing down that old house, rebuilding and then moving on — you had better make sure you don't get involved with him. It wouldn't be fair to Emma."

Despite her indignation with her mother's insinuations, her words plucked at Claire's insecurities, making them hum.

Her mother placed her hands on Claire's shoulders. "I'm only trying to take care of you. You're my daughter and I feel like we never took as good care of you or Tess as we should have. Your father and I… well… we made mistakes. And that wasn't fair to you. I guess I don't want you to do the same." Then she gave Claire a quick hug and walked toward her own car, parked beside Claire's.

Claire followed a few steps behind, got in her car and waited for her mother to leave before she reversed and drove away.

The entire drive to her place, or rather, Nik's place, her head buzzed as thoughts and questions chased each other in a futile frenzy.

"Will Nik be at the house?" Emma asked from the back seat of the car.

"No, he won't be. I told you he was gone. That's why we're doing manicures tonight." Claire flicked her hand at Mooch who was nudging aside her hair with his cold, wet nose. "Can you please hang onto Mooch? I don't want him bothering me while I drive."

Emma pulled Mooch back, reprimanding him. "When will Nik be back?"

"I'm not sure." She didn't like her vague answers any more than Emma liked receiving them.

"He won't be like my first daddy, will he? Leaving and not coming back?"

Claire's heart thumped hard and the niggling concern her mother created bloomed into panic at Emma's words. She caught herself, reminded herself of Nik's concern. Of his gentleness. He knew what was at stake for her.

And yet…

"He'll come back," Claire assured her. Though

he had seemed evasive, he had kissed her before he left. Stroked her cheek and told her he cared for her.

He wouldn't do that if he were leaving.

As she made the turn onto their street she shot a quick look back at Emma to make sure she believed what she was saying. But Emma was sitting up, looking intently ahead.

"What are those trucks doing by our house?" she asked.

Claire turned her attention back to her driving, slowing at what she saw.

A large lowboy with a track hoe was parked in front of the house and ahead of that, a dump truck.

"They're taking up our parking spot," Emma complained.

"They are indeed," Claire said, curiosity mingling with the dread she had felt just a few seconds ago.

"That's a really big whatever it is," Emma said.

"I think it's called a track hoe," Claire said.

"Maybe they're coming to tear the apartment down."

Relief surged through Claire. Of course. That would make sense.

She got out of the car, caught Mooch by the

collar and clipped his leash on before he bounded out.

"Stay close beside me," Claire cautioned Emma as they walked toward the trucks. They were still running, their diesel engines rumbling.

One of the drivers got out of the truck carrying the track hoe and ambled toward her. He wore stained coveralls with the name Norm embroidered on his chest and a worn and faded baseball cap with the logo of a sports team.

"Can I help you?" Claire asked.

"Yeah. We were told the gas company would be here to mark out the gas lines before we started taking the place down. But I don't see any flags out." Norm had a rough voice, eyebrows that met over dark brown eyes and tufts of gray hair sticking from his cap that matched his bristling mustache.

While he spoke, he pulled his cap off with one hand, scratched his head with his forefinger, then replaced it, adding a tug for good measure.

Emma had already gone into the yard and closed the gate behind her. Claire could hear Mooch barking.

"I'm sorry, I can't help you. You need to talk to the owner." She waved her hand back at the apartment building. "I can give you his number."

She called him so often when she lived there, he was on her contacts list.

"We got his number, he's not answering." Norm dropped his hands to his hips, looking over the house. "I guess we could take some of the stuff down, but I'm not sure if he wants to keep those big trees."

Claire did a double take. "Trees?" There were no trees in front of the apartment.

"I'm talking about those trees." The driver waved his arm at the large spruce and birch trees she and Tess had planted when they were young. Trees that now towered over the house, filling the front yard.

"Wait, you're here to take this house down?"

"Yeah. What did you think we were doing?"

Claire stared at him for a moment. "There has to be some mistake… Norm," Claire said, glancing at the name on his coveralls again, having forgotten it as panic rose within her.

Norm reached into his pocket and pulled out a piece of paper, unfolded and looked it over. He shook his head, then looked back at the house. "Work order says, 'dismantle and tear down of house', at this address." He waved at the house again, then showed the work order to Claire. She didn't know what to look for, but one thing stood out. On the bottom was Nik's name, printed out and his signature, or what she presumed was his signature, above it.

And right beside that was the date.

"This is dated for next week."

The guy frowned and took the paper back then shook his head. "Oh brother. I'm sorry. I got the month and day mixed up. Always was a bit dyslexic that way."

Ice slipped through her veins as he explained.

Nik was still tearing down the house despite knowing what it meant to her.

He couldn't get past what had happened here. He couldn't move on.

And if he was tearing down the house… was he still leaving?

She swallowed, looking from the house to the large track hoe to the dump truck. Sure, they were almost a week early. But still. Why hadn't Nik called her? She had stuff in the house that needed to be moved. He couldn't be that inconsiderate.

"We'll get out of your way and be back next week," Norm said. "Sorry about that. I can't believe I misread the invoice so badly."

Claire gave him a feeble smile as she pulled her phone out but nothing showed up on her screen. No message. No notification of a voice mail. She walked toward the house as the trucks shifted gears and rumbled away.

She shoved the phone back in her purse, tears threatening, anger taking place of her fear from only moments before. She should call him, but right now she was too angry.

She stalked to the house, her heartbeat gathering speed, making her feet hurry as her mind ticked over what her mother said, put it together with what she had just heard from Norm. She swallowed a knot of pain so large she was surprised she didn't choke.

Nik was following through on his initial plans.

Then he was leaving.

The two were always inextricably intertwined where he was concerned.

She swayed, pain knifing through her. What had happened between yesterday and now? How could things have changed so much?

Had they? Had he made any promises?

Claire's hands shook as she unlocked the door.

You have to fight for this house. You have to stop him.

How?

The single word reverberated through her mind. What could she do? It was his house and his plans.

She could challenge the permit. Talk to the Town Council. Tell them they had to change their mind.

As she imagined herself striding into a Council meeting, she knew how ridiculous she would sound. How little input she really had.

A vague pain flitted around her temples. Headache coming on.

Phone Nik.

Her hands trembled as she picked up her phone, but she found she couldn't do it. She was afraid of what he would tell her.

Suddenly she was tired of fighting. Tired of trying to make things work.

Maybe Tess was right. Maybe she was making too much of the house too.

However Nik's plans showed that he wasn't moving on or changing. Still bitter and still determined to erase his past rather than deal with it.

And she couldn't bear to watch that anymore.

She needed to leave, she told herself. Move on. Start over. If Nik was still tearing down the house, he was probably still leaving and she wasn't putting herself or Emma through that again.

CHAPTER 11

"This looks like a fun place to stay." Emma dropped onto one of the couches, bouncing up and down.

"It's not large, but it could work for you until you find something more permanent." Sheryl stood in the middle of the cabin, holding her son Nathaniel in her arms, frowning as she looked around the space.

After finding out about Nik's plans for the house, his plans for his trip, Claire needed to get away from the house. She called her father, who told her he would take care of everything. Claire dropped Emma off at Tess's place and within half an hour trucks were at the house. Jace, Matthew and her father helped her pack and load up. No questions were asked so Claire suspected her mother had told her father about her concerns.

Her father had called Allen Andrews about potential places for Claire to stay. There was nothing in town. Motels were all full. But Allen was Mark Andrews' brother and Mark was partners with Nate Krickson, who said he had a solution.

And through Sweet Creek's convoluted grapevine, Claire and Emma ended up in a cabin tucked in the trees behind Nate and Elise Krickson's home; on a ranch twenty miles from town.

"I truly appreciate you letting us stay here," Claire said.

"Thank Nate and Elise," Sheryl replied. "This place is on their ranch."

"I certainly will," Claire said.

"I hope you're okay here," Sheryl said. "I know it's not as big as the house you were staying in."

"It's perfect," Claire assured her, thankful that no one, not even her father, had quizzed her about her sudden move.

The cabin had one bedroom with a queen-sized bed. The main living area held two couches flanking a small wood stove, a table with four chairs and a counter with a sink, stove and refrigerator. It was cozy and under any other circumstances Claire would have loved staying there. But her heart ached, and her mind was a whirl of questions and thoughts she couldn't stop.

"We've fixed it up since I used to live here," Sheryl said, smiling as she fussed with the cloth on the table. "It's nice to have a place for company to stay."

"You used to live here?" Emma asked, leaning her elbows on the back of the couch. "I thought you were married to Mr. Mark and lived on his ranch."

"I am now, but before that, I lived here. I grew up on this ranch and when I was little, sometimes I would stay here overnight."

Emma heaved out a big sigh. "This is a fun place, but I wish we could stay at our house."

Claire didn't bother to correct her. "I do too, but like I told you. Mr. Nik wants to do something to the house and we'll be in the way." It was the best explanation Claire could give under the circumstances. Some day she would have to explain Nik's absence but until she could do it without crying, she would wait.

"We're far away from school," Emma said.

"I know it's not close to town," Sheryl put in. "But the roads are good. Mostly it's only a half an hour drive. But that depends on who is driving."

“That’s close enough.” Claire forced another smile as she looked back at Sheryl. The location wasn’t ideal, but it was a place to stay. And for that she was thankful.

Plus, it was also a half an hour drive away from Nik.

“Okay. I guess we can stay here,” Emma said, hopping up from the couch. "Does Marla live next door?"

"Actually, she does," Sheryl said sounding surprised. "How do you know her?"

"We play on the same baseball team," Emma said trying out the other couch.

“Then you girls can practice together," Sheryl said.

"I was practicing yesterday with Nik. But he's gone now," Emma said. "And my mom is not happy."

Claire made no eye contact with Sheryl, not sure she wanted to delve into anything connected to Nik. Her emotions were too shaky.

"Well that's good, then you and Marla can help each other." Sheryl gave Nathaniel another hitch, settling him higher on her hip.

The door behind them opened, and Sheryl's husband, Mark, brought in two more boxes. Sheryl's step-brother, Nate, was right behind him carrying another.

"Where should we put these?" Mark asked looking around the cabin.

Déjà vu all over again, Claire thought. Wasn't that long ago she was moving these very boxes holding the same possessions from the apartment into the house she had hoped would be hers.

She forced her tired and aching head to answer. "Just set them by the couch," she said waving toward where Emma sat.

They nodded, and he and Mark set the boxes on top of the ones already there. She had tried to decide which of the boxes stored in the old Blatchford home should come here and which would join the rest of her belongings still in storage.

Stuff she had hoped to move into the house.

She had to stop thinking about it. She had to stop thinking about Nik. Time to look ahead, not behind.

"Are you sure you don't want a hand unpacking boxes?" Sheryl asked. "Elise and I can help you."

Claire shook her head. "Thanks for the offer, but I would just as soon do it on my own. That way I know where everything is."

Besides, she wasn't sure how much to unpack. She wasn't sure how long she would stay there.

"If you need to use your phone, just come to the house," Nate said. "Our cell reception can be spotty. We have a landline at the house."

"I appreciate that," Claire said, forcing another smile. She could make all her necessary phone calls from the cafe.

“You’re sure you don’t need help?” Sheryl asked again.

Mark slipped his arm around his wife’s shoulders.

“I think Claire and Emma could use some time alone,” he said.

“Of course. It’s been a busy afternoon and night.”

Sheryl gave her a gentle smile, then with the waggle of her fingers at Emma, Sheryl, Mark, and Nate left the cabin. Mooch was tied up outside, but he was quiet.

They were finally on their own.

And Claire was exhausted. The past few hours had been a blur of instructions, directions and decisions. And sorrow. Too much sorrow.

She wanted nothing more than to crawl into bed, pull the covers over her head and feel sorry for herself. And cry.

She shook that off. After Lance, she promised herself she would never cry over a man again. She had come close to breaking that promise several times today.

"Hey, sweetheart, I think it's time for bed for you."

"I'm not that tired," Emma said. "I think we should phone Nik. I want to know why he wasn't home."

"We're not calling Nik." The comment came out harsher than she intended. Thankfully, Emma's only response was a yawn. Definitely bed time.

"C'mon, missy. It's been a long, tiring day."

Claire had packed their toiletries and necessities in a couple of suitcases so that was all handy. The bathroom was small, but adequate and moments later, Emma was tucked into the bed.

"Are you coming to bed, too?" Emma asked.

"I need to unpack a few things yet."

"It's really quiet here." Emma folded her hands on her chest, her eyes wide. "Will the cougars and coyotes howl tonight?"

"I don't know if cougars howl, but we might hear some coyotes."

"They won't come into the yard will they?"

"We have Mooch tied up outside. He'll bark if they get close and scare them away."

Emma blinked, digesting this information. Claire didn't blame her for being concerned. It *was* quiet at the Krickson ranch. Quieter than living on her parents' acreage. There, one could still hear the mournful echo of the train horn sounding through the valley.

Claire said prayers with Emma and her heart only jumped a little when her daughter asked God to bless Nik and take care of him wherever he was.

She closed the door to the bedroom, trudged over to the couch and dropped onto it with a heavy sigh. She rested her head against the back of the couch, her mind a whirl of thoughts and emotions.

Now that she was by herself, it was harder to fight back the tears.

Why had Nik done that in such a terrible manner? Why hadn't he told her about his plans before she got involved with him?

That was probably why he'd left town. He didn't want to face her.

She dragged her hands over her face, massaging her temples, hoping to ease her headache.

"Now what am I supposed to do, Lord?" she

whispered, wondering if God was paying attention.

How could things have changed so badly so quickly?

She toed her running shoes off her tingling feet letting them fall onto the floor with a clunk, swung her legs up on the couch and laid back.

As she stared up at the ceiling, the tears she promised she would not shed welled up and slid into her hair. She pressed her fingers against her lips, holding back a sudden sob.

And as she lay there she released scattered prayers, not sure what to ask for.

The only thing she knew for sure was that she had Emma to take care of and a café to run. And if she didn't get some sleep, she couldn't do either properly.

She got ready for bed, and crawled in with her daughter, pulling her close.

"How long are we staying here?" Emma whispered as they snuggled.

"Until we find a proper place to stay," Claire said.

"Like the house once Nik has it fixed up."

Claire stroked her daughter's head, threading her fingers through her hair. She wasn't sure what to say. If she told Emma the truth right then, she would be upset and not settle down at all.

"You don't have to worry about the house," was all Claire could manage. "We'll be just fine."

Thankfully her daughter trusted her, gave another yawn, and Claire felt Emma's body grow heavier before her breaths came in slow and deep.

Claire thought she would lay awake, worrying. But exhaustion wrapped its fingers around her and drew her down into blessed sleep as well.

* * *

SHE WASN'T HERE.

The house was empty; all the boxes were gone and all their clothes were packed up.

Nik stood inside the echoing house, his hands on his hips as he looked around trying to figure out what had happened. He had just tried to text Claire, but nothing came back.

He called Cory, but she couldn't help at all. She didn't know where Claire had gone or why.

He thought to call Tess, but he wasn't sure he wanted to face her. Not after the warning she gave him.

Nik went upstairs, even though he knew it

was pointless. He thought they might have left something behind, some clue as to what had happened. A note.

But all the rooms were empty. If it wasn't for the faint smell of supper from yesterday, and remnants of Claire's perfume in the bathroom, it would seem no one had lived there for years.

Where had she gone, and why hadn't she said anything to him? No text message. No note. Nothing. He trudged downstairs and dropped onto the couch, glaring around the empty room. Two days ago, when he left for Calgary he had been happier than he had been for years. He had plans — long-term plans — and hope.

And woven through all those plans was Claire and her delightful daughter.

He had been so excited to come back, to talk to her about the house, and the vision he had for it. But how could he talk when she wasn't answering his calls and hadn't even had the courtesy to tell him she was leaving.

You've been a fool. You've been taken. You've been abandoned again.

The harsh words slammed through his brain, pushing at his dreams and hopes. He didn't want to believe it, but the evidence was right in front of him. He'd be a bigger fool if he didn't pay attention to that.

Yanking his phone out of his pocket, he tried one more time to call Claire. And this one was sent straight to voicemail too. Clearly she was avoiding him.

He pushed himself off the couch, tired of inaction. He strode out of the house through the kitchen, slamming the door behind him. Once inside his truck, he reversed, then and headed down the street. He drove past the café with the slim hope it might still be open, that either Tess or Claire might still be there.

To his surprise, a faint light glowed through the window. He parked his truck, got out and walked to the door, cupping his hands around his eyes and peering inside. A shadow moved across a wall. Someone was inside.

Was it Claire?

Without stopping to think, he hammered on the door. The shadow grew larger, and then a woman walked towards him.

Tess.

She flung a towel over her shoulder, unlocked the door and let him in.

But the set of her jaw, and her narrowed eyes weren't encouraging.

"I'm looking for Claire. Do you know where she is?"

Tess folded her arms over her chest, tilting her head to one side as if studying him like he was some kind of creature that had just crawled out from under a rock.

"She asked me not to say anything to you."

"Did she tell you why? Did she tell you what was going on?"

"The only thing she said was that you lied to her. So right about now I am not telling you anything about my sister or my niece."

Her defensive posture and the belligerence in her voice revealed that he wouldn't get anywhere with her either.

The turmoil and frustration he felt morphed into anger.

"What did she say I lied to her about?"

"That's all she told me."

Nik clenched his hands at his sides. His anger shifted, swirling into confusion edged with fear.

"And you won't tell me where she is."

Tess shook her head and Nik knew he would get nothing more out of her.

"I care about her," he said. As soon as he spoke the words, he regretted letting them come out. He hated appearing vulnerable; appearing weak. But he couldn't stop himself where Claire was concerned. He'd planned on shifting his whole life around for her, and she didn't have the decency to tell him where she was or why she'd left. And why would she leave a house she was so attached to?

"I think she cared about you as well." Tess spoke the words with a grudging tone, as if she regretted telling him that much.

Nik caught the past tense of the word she used. Cared.

He gave Claire's sister a curt nod, then strode out of the café.

He got into his truck and drove back to the house. Once inside his trailer, he sat in his easy chair and looked at his surroundings. This was supposed to only be temporary. And the last few weeks he'd dared to dream about living in another place,

With Claire and Emma.

He picked up his phone again and dialed Chance's number. He answered on the first ring.

"So, was Claire surprised at what you told her?" Chance asked.

"She's not here."

"Seriously? What happened? I thought you told her about your plans."

"I have no idea what happened." Nik massaged the bridge of his nose, trying to corral his runaway thoughts. "When I left here I thought everything was good between us. I come back, and she's gone. And I don't know where she is."

"That sucks. You sure you didn't tell her something she could have taken the wrong way?"

Nik's mind went back over his last few conversations with Claire. He thought of the last kiss they shared before he left. How he held her close, and she had wrapped her arms around him. It was like they were one person, moving in the same direction.

And now?

Another woman, leaving you in the dust. Leaving you behind. Abandoning you again.

"You'd think I would be used to this," Nik said.

"So what are you going to do now?" Chance asked.

Nik heaved out a heavy sigh. "I'm not sure."

"So do you still want me to come down there? Help you out?"

"I don't know if I'm doing the work I arranged."

When he left Sweet Creek, he was full of ideas. When he talked about buying this house, with Alan Andrews, the real estate agent told him about a parcel of land on the edge of town that was for sale. The owner lived in Calgary, an elderly man, who just wanted a fair price for it. Nik had gone to talk to him, making plans for a potential subdivision. He had convinced Chance to come in with him, start a new construction company. There was work in town, and he could set up a business here.

"It was a good plan," Chance said. He sounded disappointed, and Nik felt bad that he had raised his hopes, only to dash them.

Chance had been trying for several years to find something that would give him some independence from his father-in-law. Nik thought this was the perfect opportunity.

"I'm so sorry about this, buddy," Nik said. "I hope you didn't burn any bridges with your father-in-law."

"If I did, those are bridges I should have burned years ago. I'm a free agent now and it feels good. So even if you're not following through on your original plan, I'd still like to come and help you out."

"That would be great."

"We could still make some short-term schedule," Chance said. "Maybe find a way to make enough money to take that vacation we talked about."

Nik was silent a moment.

"You hesitating? Seriously? You were ragging on me so bad about ducking out on you and now you're the one who wants to bail?" Behind the chiding words Nik heard his friends' teasing tone.

"Yeah, well, it doesn't hold as much appeal as it used to."

"Because of Claire?"

"I told you she's not in the picture."

"But she still has an effect, right?"

Nik wanted to refute that idea but was stuck. Every time he drove past Coffee Creek his heart flipped over. So he found detours and other ways to get through town. Every time he saw a woman with brown hair glinting with gold highlights, his breath shifted.

Yeah. She still had an effect.

"You sounded pretty stoked about this girl," Chance continued. "I haven't heard you this happy for a long time."

"It was the happiest I'd been in a long time." Nik stopped there. He was falling into the futility of self-pity.

"Anyway, I'm sorry about this," Nik said. "I

thought I could make a go of all of this. Really thought I could make this place a home. Set something up for both of us."

"Maybe you just need to talk to her, man."

"I would if I could get a hold of her, but I can't. So I guess that tells me enough right there." Nik scratched his forehead, not sure what his next step was. "I'll have to figure out a way to get rid of this house. It needs work, so maybe I'll do that before I go." Part of him wanted to just get up and walk away. But he needed to get as much money out of his house as he could.

If he kept himself busy, he didn't think it would be too hard to avoid Claire. He could spend a bit of time with his mother and his sister, get the work done on the house, and in a few weeks be on his way. Money in his pocket, and nothing ahead of him but sun and sand…

And what else?

"So you don't need to come out, I guess was what I was trying to say."

"I'll come anyway. There's nothing for me here. But in the meantime, you know I'll be praying for you."

"Appreciate that, man. That means a lot."

"You can pray for yourself too," Chance said.

"I might do that." His foster mother always

told him to take everything that worried or concerned him to God in prayer. He had a lot of worries and concerns. It would be a busy night.

He said goodbye to his friend and set the phone aside. He walked into the bedroom of the trailer, dropping onto the bed. Pulling open the drawer of the bedside table, he drew out the Bible his foster mother gave him when he first came into her house.

He stretched out on the bed, the Bible in his hand. Paging through it, not sure what he was looking for, he hoped he would find something to give him some comfort and strength. Hoping what he found could help him ease the anger that had ruled his life so long.

Anger he wanted to be done with.

CHAPTER 12

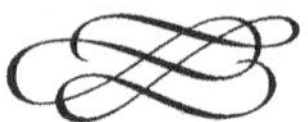

Claire let herself into the café, her feet heavy, her heart heavier. She needed to work. It was the only thing that would keep her going.

That morning, when she had woken up in the cabin — Emma snuggled up against her in bed — Claire was disoriented. Once she realized where she was, reality returned like a blast of icy water.

Despite knowing exactly how she felt about the house, Nik was still tearing it down. And he was leaving.

He couldn't, or wouldn't, let go of the pain in his life. She and Emma weren't a consideration at all.

How could it all have gone so wrong so quick?

What had she done to make him change his mind?

But no sooner was that question formulated than dismissed. She refused to take responsibility for his actions. She had simply been a woman who thought her life was changing for the better.

The back door opened, bringing in a cool draft of fall air before it was closed.

"Hey sis, how are you doing?" Tess came to stand beside her and slipped her arm across Claire's shoulders, giving her a quick sideways hug.

Claire had been holding it all in up until then. The sorrowful look her mother gave her when she dropped Emma and Mooch off was almost her undoing but for Emma's sake she managed to keep it together. Now, alone in her cafe, with her sister, the tears prickled her eyes and sorrow tightened her throat.

"Not great," she said. She pulled in a shuddering sigh and then another, frustrated that she fell apart so easily.

"Have you tried to call Nik?"

Claire shook her head, grabbing a clean bandana from her cupboard. "I don't know what to say that I haven't already said."

"Well, you could hear his side of the story."

Claire busied herself with tying her hair back then pulled in a heavy sigh. "I know his side of the story. I've heard it multiple times. He can't get past, well, the past. And the fact that that's more important to him than how I feel is hard to take."

She plugged in the dough mixer, getting ready to make the buns and bread for the day.

As she turned to get her measuring cups she saw Tess looking at her, frowning.

"What?" she asked.

"Nothing." Tess shook her head, then turned away from her sister and flicked on the coffee pot.

"It's not nothing," Claire said. "You looked like you wanted to tell me something."

"You wouldn't like it." Tess turned back to Claire, resting her hands on the counter behind her.

"Tell me anyway." Anything Tess had to say couldn't be worse than her own thoughts of the past twenty-four hours.

Tess held Claire's gaze a moment.

"Just say it, already," Claire said. "I won't cry."

"Okay. Why did you think you needed to run away when you found out Nik was tearing the house down, after all?"

"You know why. He knows exactly how I feel

about the house. What it means to me. The fact that he wants to tear it down anyway hurts."

"But there's more. Otherwise you would be going to the house to talk to him. Find out why he's doing this."

"I know why he's doing this and it's hard to watch. I know the past is eating him alive. I thought he was moving on from that. Thinking of sticking around." Her voice wavered a moment before she swallowed the emotion down. "I've been through that misery before. A man who can't let go of the past. I'm not doing that to myself anymore."

"Do you think that was all that Andy was dealing with?"

"I know it was. And I see Nik clinging to the same anger and pain."

Tess tapped her fingers against the cupboard, not meeting her sister's eye. "Memories are a tricky thing. You never know when they'll rise up from the place you thought you'd buried them. I don't know if you ever get past those hard moments," Tess finally said. "Or if you just get used to having the memories around. Or if they slowly get replaced by better ones."

Claire weighed her sister's comments. Understanding where Tess was coming from, yet fighting her resistance to what Nik was dealing with.

"I know you won't like to hear this," Tess said. "But I wonder if you're not doing the same thing?"

"What do you mean?" Claire asked.

"You are hanging pretty hard onto your memories, too. Memories of the house and what life was like when we lived there, and though they're good ones for you, they might not be correct."

"That was the happiest time of our family's life," Claire said, not understanding why her sister wasn't helping her out. "The happiest time in my life."

Tess gave her a sad smile. "Things haven't been easy for you for a while now, have they?"

Claire sucked in a breath, determined not to feel sorry for herself. "Lance sure didn't make it any easier."

"He certainly had his issues, didn't he?"

"And that's why I'm not going through this again. I don't want to be with someone who spends so much time in the past that they think they need to do the most drastic thing to get rid of it. Andy walked away from me and Emma. Nik... well..."

"He's tearing down your dream house. Disregarding your feelings."

"You sound a bit cynical. You know what that house means to me. We both grew up there, doesn't it bother you that a perfectly good house is getting torn down because a man can't get over his past?"

"You've always been so sentimental about that place. As if it holds nothing but happy times—"

"You can't say it doesn't for you," Claire interrupted.

Tess stopped a moment, biting her lip, thinking. Finally, she spoke up. "Do you know that to be true, or is that just your perception of the situation?"

"What do you mean 'perception'? There's no perception. We laughed a lot more there. We were all happier. When we moved to that glass and brick thing Mom and Dad live in now, they fought all the time."

"I loved our time in that old house. And because you're older than me, I have to trust your memories." Tess was quiet a moment clutching her mug, her shoulders hunched in a defensive posture. "But not all my memories of that house are wonderful. Mom and Dad fought in that house, too."

"What? When?" Claire asked, shocked that her sister would say such a thing.

"Remember that time we had early dismissal from school, because one of the pipes burst in the bathrooms?"

Claire frowned, dredging up the memory. "Yeah. I was allowed to go to Stephanie's place an hour earlier than we had figured on, so I was pretty excited. Where are you going with this?"

"You went to Steph's, but I went home. And Dad was there, which was unusual because he was always in the store that time of the day. I remember coming up the walk and hearing yelling. It was Mom and Dad having a huge fight."

Claire gasped. "That was two years before we moved."

"Yep. I sat on the front step, waiting for them to settle down. I didn't know if I dared go in the house, they were so angry with each other. Then Dad came storming out of the house and around the corner. He didn't see me, but I saw him stomping down the street, his hands clenched into fists. I went for a long walk around the block before I came back and went inside."

Claire considered this a moment, not sure what to think of it. "But I don't remember them fighting after that."

"Maybe not all the time, but after that I paid more attention to how they interacted. A few digs here and there which were supposed to be funny but weren't. Comments Dad made about Mom's spending. I don't think things were so fantastic in their marriage even before they built that house. Maybe they thought that the new place on the acreage would make a difference."

"Instead, they ended up arguing more," Claire said with a sigh. She chewed her lip, still trying to process what her sister had told her. "You never told me about the fight."

"I didn't want to talk about it to anybody. And when I came in the house, Mom was acting as if nothing happened. It seemed weird to bring it up." She gave Claire a careful smile. "I didn't think to mention it until now."

"So you think I'm being overly romantic about that house?"

"I think you're pinning too many hopes on it. I think you're hoping it will make the home that you've been desperately trying to create for Emma when all it is, really, is just a building."

"I'm not the only one doing that." Claire released a harsh laugh. "Emma seems to think that if Nik and I get together all her problems will be solved. She's got this idea that he will be her new dad."

"And will he?"

Claire was about to vehemently deny it. And yet, the kisses they shared, the moments they'd spent together, the conversations they had made her stop short of denial. She and Nik had been moving closer and closer and Claire had allowed herself some dreams.

"You're hesitating. If you weren't thinking about it, you wouldn't be hesitating. Talk to him. Again. Let him know exactly what's on the line with you." Tess took a sip of her coffee then drew in a long breath. "And then, while you're doing that, ask yourself why you're hanging onto something he needs to dump. Why you are making this house the symbol of your happily-ever-after. Why you can't let go of your dreams to help him find his?"

"Because I'm unsure of what his dreams are. He always said that when he tore down the house he would build his fourplex and leave. You know I have to be responsible. I have to be careful with Emma. I don't dare bring someone into her life who might leave again."

"And then you're back to the beginning," Tess said quietly. "I think the problem is neither of you are willing to take that first step. Both of you have been hurt in the past and are both protecting yourselves."

"Like I said, I'm not just thinking about me; I have Emma to think about. She's my first priority."

"And your heart?"

Claire bit her lips, fighting down the pain that had dogged her all day. "That's not fair."

"Do you care for him?"

"Too much."

"Then maybe find a way to convince him to stay."

Claire held that thought a moment but shook her head. "I went running after Lance. I cried in front of him, pleading with him to come back. I'm not doing that again."

Tess stared at her. "I… I didn't know. You never said."

"It wasn't something I was proud of, that's for sure." She drew in a steadying breath. "So. That's that. And we better get going on the food for the day."

* * *

"Can we go see Nik today?" Emma asked as

Claire pulled up to her mother's place on Thursday morning.

"No, honey. I told you, he's busy."

"I don't like it that he's so busy. I don't like it that we can't see him." Emma pouted as she grabbed her knapsack and got out of the car.

Mooch jumped out behind her, thankfully waiting while Claire clipped his leash onto his collar.

"I know, honey, and I'm sorry, but he will let us know when it works for us to see him."

Though it had only been a couple of days since everything in her life fell apart, it seemed like months. She had kept herself busy, forcing herself to do one thing, then the next.

Thankfully, Tess hadn't asked Claire anything more about Nik.

Thankfully, Nik hadn't stopped by the coffee shop.

Thankfully Emma only asked a couple of times each day about Nik and when they would see him.

It was as if the prayers she'd been sending up for peace were being answered.

Then why did her heart hurt so much? Why did thoughts of Nik make her feel as if all light was bleached out of her life?

She felt as if she were simply going through the motions of living. Doing what needed to be done. Trying not to think too far ahead. She and Emma couldn't stay in the cabin forever. Winter was coming and when the snow fell she knew her little car would have trouble on the country roads.

She had scoured the papers the last couple of days looking for a place to rent, hoping, praying something would come up.

But nothing had.

"I don't want to go to school today," Emma sighed, dragging her backpack on the ground behind her while Mooch tried to grab it with his teeth.

Claire reached over and caught the backpack rather than nag Emma, again, about how to properly carry it.

"I'm sorry, honey, but you have to. You know that," Claire said as she knocked on the door and pulled it open. Mooch barreled in ahead of them and ran to the large, stone fireplace, falling down on the bed in front of it. "Besides, you don't want to fall behind your classmates, do you?"

"Billie was teasing me again. About not having a daddy. I told him I was going to get one." Emma looked directly at Claire as she knelt to take off

Emma's jacket. "Am I, Mom? Will Nik be my daddy?"

Claire bit her lip, wishing Emma wouldn't talk like that. She had tried to discourage it repeatedly, but her daughter clung to the idea.

Just as Claire was struggling to find the right way to tell Emma it wasn't happening, her father joined them.

"Grandpa. Yay," Emma cried out, wriggling away from her mother. She threw herself at her grandfather who swung her up into his arms, then grunted.

"You're getting too big to do that," he said, giving her a quick hug then setting her down.

"I'm still a little girl," Emma protested, leaning against him.

Her father stroked Emma's hair, then gave Claire a vague smile. "So, how are you settling into the cabin?"

"It's just temporary."

"Grandma is in the kitchen, Emma," her father announced, patting Emma on the head. "Why don't you go see what she's making?"

Emma nodded and skipped off, at peace with the world again.

As her father turned to her, Claire looked more closely at him, trying to blend what Tess had said with what she'd seen. Had she truly been so blind all those years, thinking her parents were happy when, maybe, they'd been fighting the entire time?

"Was there something you needed to talk about?" Claire said, beating him to the punch.

"Actually, there is." Her father tapped his fingers against the side of his leg. "The last couple of days Emma has been talking about Nik. Telling us that he was supposed to be her father, but that she isn't sure anymore. I know your mother talked to you about this, but it disturbs us that this continues."

"I can't stop that. You know Emma. She has her own mind, but Nik will not be her father." She spoke the words with finality. It was as if she had to convince herself as much as her father.

"That's good to know. I hear he's tearing down the house. I know that makes you sad, but I don't want you to get your hopes up about him."

"Don't worry about me, Dad. I have no hopes where Nik is concerned." She clamped her trembling lips together, fighting down the clench of sorrow. Saying the words aloud made them more real.

"Well I'm glad to hear that." Her father patted her on the shoulder in an awkward gesture. He was never a demonstrative person when it came to affection.

Claire was about to leave, but then stopped, her hand on the doorknob. "Tess told me something about you and Mom in the other house. She said you guys also used to fight when we lived there."

Her father looked pained and ran his hand through his hair. "Well, now, that's not entirely true. But…" He seemed to fumble trying to find the right words.

"I know you guys fought a lot here."

"I'm sorry you had to witness that." Her father grabbed the back of his neck, massaging it. "Things haven't been easy here. But you need to know that your mother and I are in a better place now. You know we've been going for counseling and that's helped a lot."

"So you guys were having problems in the other house already?"

"Why are you asking these questions?" Her father asked. "It was in the past, and we've moved on from there."

"I don't know." Claire heaved out another sigh. "I think I wove too many dreams around that other house, and I'm just trying to be realistic. I thought we were happy there."

"I think we were," her father assured her. "But like any family, we had our difficulties." He then gave her a puzzled frown. "Where are you going with this?"

Claire gave him a sad smile. "Tess told me I was unrealistic about our life in that house. That I always thought we were happier there than we were here."

"It's not the house that makes or breaks the family," her father said, his voice quiet. "It's the people *in* it that make it a home. I think everywhere we lived we tried to make a home for you girls. Maybe not always successfully, but we sure tried. This house," he spread his hand out indicating the large open space they stood in, "was just another building. A place to live. Just like the other place was. The other house didn't make us happy, and this house didn't make us happy, we were the ones who needed to create that happiness. It took a lot of prayers, and a lot of work, but that's what any relationship is about. It also took a lot of sacrifices and swallowing of pride. We moved out of that house because we wanted to give you girls a better place to live in. Both me and your mother. Maybe it was a mistake, but everything we did, we did for your sake."

"But I never wanted to move here," Claire said.

"You would say that," her father said. "Yet you are the one who played outside here the most. Remember that fort you made in the trees in the back? And that skating rink we made for you? That all happened here. I think you were happy here, too."

Claire let the memories her father mentioned sink into her mind. Then she released a hard laugh. "I wanted to do the same thing you did for us. I want to make a good place for Emma. I want to give her a home. Actually, I wanted to give her that house. The house I used to live in."

"I know you. You'll make a home anywhere you go," her father said, patting her once again on the shoulder. "You're a good mother. You've done amazingly well with the hand you've been dealt. Your mother and I are very proud of you and are so thankful for Emma. I know you didn't choose what happened to you, but you made the best of it."

Her father's praise warmed her heart. And threatened to make her weepier than she felt.

She gave him a quick hug, then approached the door. "I should get going. Tess is probably at the café looking at the clock and wondering where I am."

"And that's something else we're so happy about." Her father said. "How you and your sister get along. It's also a real blessing to me and your mother."

Claire gave him another smile and stepped out the door, closing it carefully behind her. She looked over the yard, trying to see it with different eyes. She saw a tree, with the rope hanging down from it yet. Remnants of the swing she and her father had set up. A bare patch of grass further down showed her where the old skating rink used to be.

Despite her roiling emotions, she smiled. She had some happy memories here. And her father was right. It wasn't the house that made the home, it was the people who lived in it.

She got into her car and drove to the café. But before she turned down Main Street, she took a detour that took her past the house. The dump had returned, and she heard the *beep beep* of the trackhoe on the other side of the house followed by the sickening crunch of lumber.

Despite what her father had told her, she couldn't stop the sharp sting of tears. Nik was going through with it. He was taking down her old home.

She couldn't bear to watch.

And yet, she slowed a moment, trying to look at it through his eyes. Trying to imagine a young boy sitting up in a room, wishing he was outside, wishing he was anywhere else but there. Wondering every day what would happen.

Her memories shifted into his and blended with what her father said.

It's not the house that makes the home, it's the people in it.

And while she understood what Nik was dealing with, at the same time, she had so hoped the three of them could find a way to get together.

He hadn't contacted her once. Hadn't connected with her to explain.

He had just shut her out.

But as she drove away, a prayer rose up in her mind.

Please Lord, be with Nik. Please let what he is doing heal him from his hurt. Please let it bring him peace.

* * *

"WE'LL NEED MORE EIGHT-BY-EIGHTS," Chance said to Nik, dropping his hammer into the metal bracket of his tool pouch. "I don't think six-by-sixes will be strong enough to hold the porch roof up."

Nik made a note on the discarded piece of plywood he used as a list. "Anything else?"

Chance rubbed his chin for a moment. "Yeah. How about a phone call to Claire?"

Nik's heart jumped at the mention of her name, but he kept his expression neutral. "I think we'll need more wood screws, too."

Chance shrugged but Nik could tell he wouldn't leave the topic alone. In fact, when he arrived last night, it was the first thing Chance had asked Nik — If he had talked to Claire.

It had been four days since Claire had left. Without even the decency of sending him a text explaining why she'd left. He shouldn't care. She was just proving herself to be no different than many of the other women in his life.

Your mother had a reason.

He held that thought a moment and sighed again. He had spent the past few evenings with Joyce and Cory, evading Cory's questions about Claire. He had finally sent a text to Cory asking her to just leave it alone. She replied with a sad face emoji, so he hoped the text had done its work.

But he and his mother were slowly making peace, growing closer even as he and Claire were moving further apart.

"What you need is to have your head screwed on," Chance said. "Seriously, just swallow your pride and call her already."

"I'm heading out now, if there's anything else you need just send me a text." Still carrying the piece of plywood, Nik got into his truck. A few minutes later he was heading down the road, trying not to think of Chance's comments. He turned down one street, slowing as he came to the intersection. A turn to the right would bring him to Claire's coffee shop. A turn to the left, to the lumber yard. And for just a moment, he slowed and wondered what to do. A quick glance at the clock showed him the time. 10:00. Things would be slowing down. Claire wouldn't be so busy.

And what would he say to her?

She was the one who left without even leaving a note.

He turned left.

But as he drove Chance's words whirled through his head. Maybe he should swallow his pride. Take the first step. Because he knew he hadn't imagined the feelings that had surged between them. The kisses they shared.

Please Lord, he prayed, turning to God, realizing how much of his life was out of his control. *Please show me what I need to do. Help me find a chance to talk to her. To find out the truth.*

CHAPTER 13

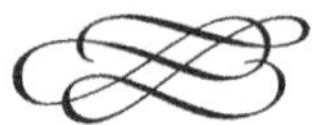

"That will be $12.55," Claire said, her smile forced as she punched the numbers into the terminal.

Nadine tapped her card on the terminal to pay and took the coffee from Tess. "So, I heard you had to move again," she said as Claire handed Nadine her order.

"Yeah. Nik Austin is tearing the house down. So it just was a matter of time." It was easier to say those words than it would have been a few days ago. Seeing the equipment in front of the house, hearing the crash of the wood had ended the dream she had clung to. She wished Nik would get the apartment done quickly so he could move on.

"Really? I was at the town office the other day for an article I'm working on, and one girl made some comment about Nik coming in. What a hassle it was to change the tear-down permit he applied for." Nadine grinned. "Of course, she did add that it wasn't such a big deal, seeing as how he was so good looking."

Claire kept her face expressionless, but even as she held Nadine's curious gaze, she wondered what changes Nik had applied for.

"Enjoy your sandwich," was all Claire said.

Once Nadine left, the store was empty of customers.

"What you think Nik was doing at the office?" Tess asked, checking Claire's reaction.

"It doesn't matter. It's none of my business anymore."

"So you haven't texted him or talked to him?"

"He hasn't called me, either."

"It's a new century," Tess said. "You don't have to wait. Besides, you're the one that took off without letting him know anything."

Claire slid open the door of the display case and pulled up the muffin tray. "I better fill this up."

"I wish you wouldn't be so stubborn." Tess

walked back to the kitchen with her. "The guy probably doesn't even know why you left."

As Tess spoke, common sense fought with the loneliness that had dogged her the last few days. And with the loneliness came the second thoughts that also plagued her. "I'm not sure what to do," she said, setting the empty muffin tray on the butcher block island. She bit her lip as she turned to her sister. "What do you think I should do?"

"I think you should go over to Nik and ask him why he's tearing down the house. What he thinks it will accomplish and if he will ever get over the pain and sorrow he feels. Just put it out there."

"And what if I don't like his answer? What if I don't like to hear him tell me he's leaving?"

"Do you like him?"

Claire held that thought a moment. "I do. But like I said, I don't think I can get involved with someone who clings too hard to the pain of the past. Someone who wants to move on."

"How do you know he does?"

"Because he told me. Often. That was his plan. And I don't want to risk putting myself, or Emma, through that again."

Tess sighed as she took a container of freshly

made muffins out of the refrigerator. "I get that. But Andy also left because he didn't want to be a father to Emma. We both know that was a factor." Tess set the muffins on the tray, glancing up at Claire as she did.

"I know."

"And Nik seems to get along with Emma, so that's not a problem for him."

Claire realized the truth of what Tess was saying. "But..."

"But what? I know you're scared. I was scared to let Jace back into my life. We don't like being vulnerable and risk being hurt. But would you sooner let him go? Let him walk out of your life and end up lonely again without giving him a chance?" The tray was full, and Tess washed her hands again. Then she picked up the tray. "It's up to you. You've taken control of many parts of your life. Take control of this part."

Claire's thoughts were a jumble of choices and concerns. Her old vulnerability returned but she could also see the truth in what Tess said.

But before she could make a decision, her phone rang.

"Maybe that's him right now," Tess said with a grin.

"Yeah, right." But despite her cynicism, she

couldn't squash a tiny flare of hope. Which turned into concern when she looked at the screen. It was the school.

"Mrs. Donnel," a voice asked. "This is Eileen from the school. We are wondering if Emma is at the cafe with you."

Claire's heart stuttered. "No. She's not. Isn't she at the school?"

"Well, it seems she's disappeared—"

"How? When?" Panic bloomed in her chest, spreading icy pulses through her body.

"She was out for recess, then, when it came time to bring them all in, she wasn't present and accounted for."

"She's not here. Is she at my parent's?"

"No. She's not."

"Did you call the police?"

"That was our first call, but they asked us to check with you. Please, understand, we had no idea—"

"Find her," Claire blurted out. "Find her now."

"We will. Please, again—"

But Claire stabbed at the screen before she could hear another apology. Her heart was racing, blood pounded her temples, panic clung to her heart. Had she been kidnapped? Lost?

And what could she do?

Tess came back just as Claire was yanking her jacket off the hook at the back of the store.

"What's up?" Tess asked. "You look terrified."

"The school just called. Emma didn't come in after recess. I'm going to look for her."

"Did they call the cops?"

"Yes."

"Is she at Mom and Dad's?"

"Apparently not." Claire struggled to button her coat with her hands trembling.

Tess came close and caught Claire's hands. "Maybe you should stay here. In case she comes here. You can't go running off, willy-nilly to look for her. If the police are involved, they're better equipped than you are."

Claire bit her lip, fear pounding a threatening rhythm. "But I don't know what else to do."

"I think it's best you wait here for a few minutes at least. Just to make sure she's not trying to come here. If she doesn't come then we can shut the cafe down and go out looking for her."

She couldn't argue with the sense of that, but at the same time, her mother's heart wanted to be doing something. Anything.

"Okay. I'll give her another ten minutes but then I'm going looking."

And while she waited, she knew she had another call to make.

* * *

"So, you're loaded up and ready to go."

Skip Moore handed Nik his copy of the bill and with a wave of thanks, Nik climbed back into his truck.

As soon as he pulled away from the lumberyard, his phone rang.

His heart gave a renegade skip. Ever since Claire left, every time his phone rang, he wondered if it was her.

But it was only Chance.

"So… we've got a small problem here," Chance said, morosely.

"Define 'problem.'" He almost rolled his eyes. Ever since he started work on the house it seemed like one problem led to another problem. Not for the first time he wondered if he was doing the right thing.

"There's a little girl here. She's crying and she's mad at me because I tore the porch down. I have no idea what she's talking about, but she's semi-hysterical. Gotta help me out bro. I don't do little kids." Chance sounded positively fearful.

"Is her name Emma?"

He heard Chance's muffled voice, then he came back. "Yeah that's what her name is. And she's saying something about a daddy. I dunno. I'm kind of lost here, buddy."

What was Emma doing at the house? She was supposed to be in school. On the tails of that thought came a surge of panic. What was she doing all the way over there? Did Claire know what was going on?

"I'll be right there." He ended the call and stepped on the gas, heading back to the house. As he did his phone rang again. He clicked the button on the steering wheel to connect the call to hands-free

"Nik? This is Claire. I'm calling about Emma. I just got a call from the school that she's gone. Do you have any idea where she is?" Claire sounded frantic. Nik didn't blame her. A parent's worst nightmare; a missing child.

"Well my partner just called. Apparently, she's at the house. I'm heading over there right away."

"Oh, thank you, Lord," Claire said, her voice breaking. "I'm coming too."

"I'm not far from the coffee shop, I can pick you up." As soon as he spoke the words, he wondered if he'd made the right choice.

But he had a frantic mother, and a child who decided to run away on his hands. Now was not the time for personal feelings.

When he pulled up in front of the café, Claire was on the street, her arms wrapped around her midsection, like she could hold herself together that way. He reached over and opened the door to his truck and she jumped in. She wore her usual bandana, and stained apron. Her eyes were wide, her cheeks flushed, and she looked frightened half to death.

"I think she's okay," was all Nik could say to assure her. "Chance didn't seem too fussed, other than he had to watch a little girl."

Claire clenched her hands in her lap, her knuckles white. She shot him a quick glance, fear etched into her gentle features.

So much had happened between them, but Nik still reached across the cab and covered her hands with one of his. "She's at the house and according to my partner, she's okay. We'll be there in just a few minutes."

Claire bit her lip and to his surprise, she twisted her fingers around his. They were icy cold but even that simple touch sent a flood of warmth through him.

They drove that way all the way to the house.

Holding hands, connected by their concern for Emma.

Nik drove well over the speed limit. When he got to the house, he hit the brakes, his tires screeching. And before he had shut off the truck, Claire was out the door, calling for Emma. Almost at once, her daughter came around the house running toward Claire.

Nik got out of the truck, following a little slowly. The weight on his heart lifted in relief as he saw Emma and Claire cling to one another.

She was okay.

Chance came around the house scratching his head.

"So, what happened?" Claire asked, kneeling in front of Emma with her hands on her daughter's shoulders. Claire gripped Emma tightly in a bear hug again, then pulled back, checking her over to make sure she was okay. "What were you doing coming here?"

Emma pulled in a hiccupping breath, rubbed her hand over her nose, her cheek wet with tears.

"I wanted to talk to Nik. You weren't going to, and I needed to talk to him. I was going to ask him not to tear the house down. But he started already. The house will be gone. And you're not marrying him, and he will not be my daddy. I'm so very sad." She sobbed harder, falling into Claire's arms.

Nik glanced from Claire to Emma to Chance, trying to figure out what had happened.

Chance took a step back, holding up his hands in a gesture of surrender. "I think now would be a good time for me to take a coffee break." Chance gave Emma and Claire a wide berth and held out his hand to Nik. "I'll take your truck. You go ahead and straighten this out."

As Chance took the keys, he leaned in close. "I'm gonna take my time. You get this fixed." He held Nik's eyes, his gaze hard. Steady.

Then he left.

Claire still held Emma, stroking her hair, her own cheeks glistening with tears.

Nik joined them, resting his hand on Emma's head. He wanted to pull Claire into his arms, but his emotions were jumbled right now, and a dozen questions plagued him, but he held his feelings back, if only momentarily. He didn't want to interrupt the love-fueled reunion of a mother and a daughter. Instead he called the school and the police to let them know Emma had been found. When he was done Emma had stopped crying and Claire stood, looking over at Nik.

His breath caught in his throat as their eyes met and held each other. The old feelings returned so fast, it was like he'd never been angry with her. Like she had never left.

He caught himself and took a step back to create distance between them.

Sorrow settled over her face, and he regretted the step. But he had to be firm. She still held too strong a hold on his heart.

Nik turned his attention to Emma. "Are you okay?"

Emma just nodded, then looked over at him, her expression holding the sting of accusation. "Why are you tearing down our house?"

Nik frowned, taken aback at her question. "It's just the porch, honey. We needed to take it down because it was no good."

"But you made a big mess of the back of the house," Emma said, sniffing. "And Mommy said that it doesn't matter if you take the house down, but it matters to me. I don't want you to wreck my bedroom."

Nik's confusion grew, as he tried to sort out what Emma had said.

"Did you think I was tearing down the whole house?"

“You said you would,” Emma said, her voice as accusing as her expression.

Nik allowed her words to settle for a minute, then he turned to Claire. “Is that what you thought, too?”

Claire folded her arms over her stomach. “It’s what you’ve always talked about. And I came here that one day when the track hoe and the dump truck were here. The guy showed me a work order for a teardown. For this house.”

“Was that the day you and Emma moved out?”

Claire confirmed. “I thought you were tearing the house down despite what you said. I thought you couldn’t get past what happened to you here. And I thought once you were done here, you were moving. Just like you always said you were.”

“And you probably also thought I didn’t care how you felt about the house,” Nik ventured.

Her quick glance downward indicated that he was right.

And with that one movement everything fell into place.

“I’m sorry you ended up meeting Norm. He wasn’t supposed to come at all. I cancelled that work order.”

Claire stared at him, her eyes roving over him, her brows furrowed. “But the porch…”

Nik held her puzzled gaze. "The foundation is sagging, and the roof is a mess. It's gotta come down. For safety reasons."

Claire looked from him to the house, swiping at the tears on her cheeks, still clutching Emma's hand. "So, you're not taking the house down?"

Nik took a step closer to her. "No. I'm not." He spoke quietly, afraid anything he said might send her away again. "I'm fixing it up. Got some ideas for the inside."

"And when you've fixed it up?" Claire held his gaze now and a tiny ember of hope glowed within him when he glimpsed the expectation in her eyes. "Then what?"

"I was thinking of moving in. I'll need a place to stay, after all." He watched her closely while he spoke, hoping, praying that what he had to say was what she wanted to hear.

"And why is that?" she asked. Her words were tentative.

"I've got a big job coming up here in Sweet Creek. It will take about three years and, while that's in the works, I'm sure I can get other contracts."

"So, you're staying?"

Nik laid his hand on Claire's shoulder looking deep into her troubled eyes. "I'm staying. And not just for my mother and my sister or the work I've set up." He looked down at Emma who watched the conversation between her mother and Nik with a puzzled expression. "Emma and you. You two are the main reason I want to stay."

He wished he felt as calm as he sounded. It was like walking to the edge of a cliff and turning his back to the yawning, void behind him. Completely vulnerable. All it would take was the tiniest rejection the smallest push and it would all be over. He would have gambled for nothing.

Claire blinked slowly. She was silent at first... Then a soft smile stretched her lips. Her eyes shone. But she stayed where she was.

"You're staying for us?" she asked.

"You're not moving away?" Emma squealed.

"I'm not. I figured I'd better stay close to the women I love. You and Emma."

Without hesitation, Emma launched herself at Nik, grabbing him around the waist, almost toppling him. "You're staying. You're staying." Then she pulled back looking him straight in the eye, her own narrowed as if measuring his intent. "And are you going to be my daddy?"

Claire gasped, and Nik laughed at her forthrightness.

"Emma. Please," Claire reprimanded.

"Well? Are you?"

"It depends on what your Mommy would like," was all Nik dared say.

Emma sighed, pursed her lips and twisted them to the side as she looked at Claire. "Are you going to say yes?"

Claire still looked stunned and Nik took another chance.

He took her hand pressing it between his, looking deep into her wide, surprised gaze.

"I love you, Claire. I really do. It's not a perfect love and I know I'll make mistakes, but I promise to do the best I can."

"You love me?"

Nik heard the puzzlement in her voice and for a moment he wondered if he had pushed too hard, too fast.

But then Claire squeezed his hands in return. And she pressed her other hand to her lips, as if trying to hold her emotions in.

"I really love you," Nik repeated, hoping she believed him. "I realized how much when you left. I didn't want to miss you. Didn't want to think you could hold my heart so securely. I didn't like how I felt without you."

"And what about me?" Emma asked. "Did you miss me too?" she asked.

Nik pulled his hand out of Claire's, and lifted Emma into his arms, giving her a tight hug. "I missed you so much," he said, holding her close, thankful she was okay.

Emma pulled away, her hands framing his face. "I missed you too." she repeated. "And so did my mommy. She was crying all the time at the cabin."

Emma's innocent words made Claire blush and gave Nik a surge of hope.

"She did, did she?"

"Did you cry?" Emma asked. "When we were gone?"

Nik gave her another hug, then lowered her to the ground, keeping her hand tucked in his. He took Claire's again, smiling at her.

"Yes. I was very sad. I missed you and your mother. A lot." He gave Claire's hand a tug. But it took very little encouragement for her to move toward him, to step into his one-armed embrace. He pressed a kiss to the top of her head, his heart so full he thought it would pop out of his chest.

"Can I go into the house? To make sure my room is okay?" Emma asked.

"Yes. But stay away from the kitchen and dining room, okay?" Nik told her.

"Of course. Because I don't want to go out the

back door and end up on the ground. Because there's no porch," Emma announced as she pulled away from them and ran up the front steps.

She disappeared into the house and Nik took advantage of her absence and pulled Claire into his arms again, holding her close, sharing a deep, warm kiss with her, his lips moving gently and then with more insistence.

She clung him to her, returning his kiss with an ardor that surprised and pleased him at the same time.

A passing vehicle honked at them and Nik pulled away, suddenly embarrassed.

But Claire smiled. "Probably no one important," she said. "Besides, it doesn't matter. A lot of things don't matter anymore."

"Like what?"

Still resting in his arms, she looked over at the house. "You know, I made too much of this place. Put too much pressure on it for me to give me my happy-ever-after. Well, that's what Tess told me, and she was right."

She turned back to him. "I'm sorry for not realizing what you had to deal with. I'm sorry that you went through such awful things here. I understand how you would want to erase that time from your life. So, if you want to tear the house down and start over, I'm fine with that."

Her eyes were sincere and her words gave him a freedom he hadn't felt in years.

"I mean it," she said, giving him a tiny shake as if to underline what she was saying. "The house doesn't matter. Your peace of mind and happiness does."

Nik gave her another kiss then smiled down at her, tracing her features, committing them to memory. "You know, it doesn't matter to me either. I've been looking the house over and I have a few plans for it. Some changes I'd like to make. But I want it to stay up. It has a lot of character and I want to make it our home."

She smiled at him. "Home. I love that word."

He pulled her close again, resting his head on hers, his eyes closed as his heart filled with a love he never thought he would experience.

"I do too," he whispered.

"Are you guys coming?" Emma called out from the front door. "I want to talk about my bedroom."

Nik chuckled and pulled away, still looking at Claire. "Her majesty has summoned us."

"I'm sorry—"

Nik touched her lips with his finger, smiling

as he shook his head. "You never have to apologize for her. She's a gift and a treasure." For a fleeting moment Nik thought of the child he might have had, then looked back, his heart full. "And I thank God for giving me you and her."

Claire chuckled and slipped her arm around his.

Then, together they walked toward their new home.

EPILOGUE

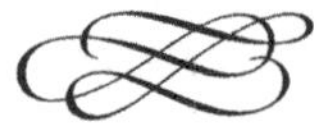

"What do you think of Oasis?" Claire held up a card, turning it to Nik, who had his arm around her shoulders, holding her close to his side.

They sat in the living room, a fire crackling in the grate. Emma had finally fallen asleep.

The scent of sawdust and drywall dust still lingered in the air. After the porch was finished, Nik had taken out the wall between the dining room and the living room, opening it up. He had finished it last week.

Once he'd declared the house habitable, Claire and Emma had moved all their things, once again, back into the house. They hadn't taken the furniture out of storage yet.

Claire wanted to paint the living and dining areas first.

He studied it a moment then shook his head. "I'll feel like I'm in a swimming pool every day."

Claire chuckled realizing he was probably right. She set the paint chip aside and pulled out another one. "Wintergreen?"

Nik scratched his face, looking rather pained.

"Another no," Claire announced.

"Well, I'm kind of okay with it. It's just kind of… well..."

"Girly. I know." She picked up another card and looked at it as well, realizing that many of the choices she had made were when she thought that only she and Emma would live in the house. Never, in all her imaginings, had she thought she would be taking a man's opinion into consideration when it came time to paint and decorate the house.

"Do you have any preferences?"

Nik scratched his forehead with his index finger, thinking. "I kind of like blueish colors."

Claire riffled through the cards and found a couple more. "How about this?"

To her relief, Nik smiled. "Yeah. I can live with that."

"That's the important part. We'll be looking at

it for a long time. I'm not a huge fan of painting, so unless we hire someone to do it next time, we'll be living with your choice for a while."

"So, 'choose wisely' is what you're saying?"

"Pretty much," she determined, chuckling.

He set the paint card aside and pulled her closer. "I don't want to talk about paint anymore."

"Okay, let's talk about the wedding."

This elicited a groan from Nik.

She laughed again but held her hand up to let the diamond on her finger sparkle in the subdued light. "I'm excited about our wedding."

"I know Chance is. For various reasons."

Nik and Chance had moved his trailer from the yard to a park not far from town and were both living in it for now.

"Only two more weeks," Claire said, still hardly daring to believe it would actually happen.

Nik gave her a gentle kiss and sighed into her hair, both arms wrapped around her.

She lay quietly in his arms, enjoying the moment. Enjoying just being with him.

"Are you going to be okay? Living here?" she asked. The question had been lying dormant since they'd patched things up. They'd been so busy they hadn't had much time to just be together. To just talk.

"I'm looking forward to making good memories here," he said quietly.

She knew there were deep sorrowful memories buried beneath his calm facade. Hard pain.

"Do you want to talk about some of the other stories?" she asked, hoping to ferret out one more sorrow that he could release into the open spaces, lay at the foot of the cross.

He shook his head and gave her a gentle smile, fingering a strand of hair away from her face.

"We have lots and lots of time to talk," he said.

"I'm always here, you know."

His smile deepened, creating an attractive fan of wrinkles around his eyes. Smile lines that she hadn't seen often.

"I know and I'm grateful for you. For all you give me. That we got pushed together."

"You do the same for me, you know. We have both benefited from everything that shifted and brought us together. I think we both needed to change our focus." She sighed, looking around the house feeling a tiny ping of sorrow, thinking of her parents fighting here. She had always surrounded and imbued that home with an aura of happiness that wasn't real.

"Where are you?"

She returned her gaze to him, releasing a

gentle sigh that carried the pain away. "I'm thinking of the home we will make here. I want to make absolute sure it's okay with you."

"I told you. It is."

His emphatic declaration told her to leave it be.

She curled back against him, her head nestled in the crook of his shoulder. Upstairs her daughter slept in Tessa's old room. Maybe, someday, there would be one or two more children to sleep in those beds, to wait for the furnace to kick in. To wait to come downstairs.

She and Nik would be there, waiting for them.

"We're going to make this a happy home," she declared. "Together."

"I like the sound of that." Nik rubbed his cheek against her head. "I know it won't always be easy and I'm sure we'll have our arguments."

"You think?" she teased.

"I know. I'm not the easiest person to live with."

"Neither am I. We're two flawed individuals with our own happy and sad stories."

"And we have the rest of our life to share them," he said. "And for that, I thank God for this place."

His sincerity was palpable. Claire's heart soared at his words.

"I do too," she said. "Because it's going to be ours. Our home. We'll make our own memories and our own mistakes. But you know," she drew back, cupping her face with her hand, "the best part is that we're not on our own. We have the prayers of family and friends holding us up. And we have each other."

Nik leaned in close and sealed her declaration with a kiss.

A noise on the stairs caught Claire's attention and she looked up to see Emma's tousled head peering down at them, her hands grasping the spindles of the bannister.

"Come down here, you little stinker," Nik said, beckoning her with a wave of his hand.

Emma didn't need another invitation. She scooted down and plopped between Nik and Claire, wiggling to make room.

The couple curled their arms around Emma, containing her, closing the circle.

"I'm happy," Emma said, quietly resting her head against Claire's, her hand holding Nik's.

"So are we, little munchkin," Nik said with a chuckle. "So are we."

"I think we should play a game," she said. Then yawned.

"How about we just sit here," Nik said. "Just enjoy the fire and the quiet."

"Just be together?" Emma sounded puzzled.

"Exactly that," Nik said, smiling at Claire. "Just be together."

"Okay."

Emma didn't sound convinced but she relaxed quietly.

Together the three of them sat and watched the fire. Making a new memory to fill the space in their house. Their home.

<<<<>>>>

I hope you enjoyed reading Claire and Nik's story and seeing him finally reunited with his sister and mother. This is the last of the Sweet Hearts of Sweet Creek for now. I hope you liked your time in this town.

Other books in the
Sweet Hearts of Sweet Creek Series:

HOMECOMING #1

HER HEART'S PROMISE #2
CLOSE TO HIS HEART#3
DIVIDED HEARTS #4
A HERO AT HEART #5

I have another series that's out now. The first book in this series is called, The Only Best Place.

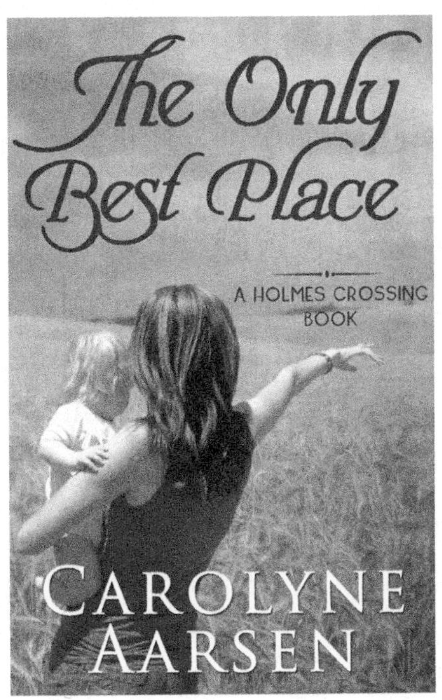

READ AN EXCERPT HERE:

SMILE. Think happy thoughts. Take a deep breath and...

"Hello. I'm Leslie VandeKeere, and I'm a farmer's wife."

No. No. All wrong. That sounds like I'm addressing a self-help group for stressed-out urban dwellers.

I angled the rearview mirror of my car to do a sincerity check on my expression and pulled a face at my reflection. Brown eyes. Brown hair. Both the polar opposite of the VandeKeere signature blonde hair and blue eyes repeated throughout the Dutch-based community of Holmes Crossing.

During the past hour of the long drive from Vancouver to here, I'd been practicing my introduction to varied and sundry members of the vast community of which I knew about four and a half people. I'd been trying out various intros. That last one was a bust. I'd never been a farmer's wife. Would never be a farmer's wife. I'm a nurse, even though my focus the next year was supposed to be on our marriage. Not my career.

I cleared my throat and tried again. "Our year here will be interesting."

Worse yet. Most women could break that code faster than you could say "fifteen percent off." *Interesting* was a twilight word that either veered toward the good or the dark side.

Right now my delivery was a quiet and subdued Darth Vader.

I had to keep my voice down so I wouldn't wake my two kids. After four *Veggie Tales* and a couple of off-key renditions of "The Itsy Bitsy Spider," they had finally drifted off to sleep, and I didn't want to risk waking them. The eighteen hour trip had been hard on us. They needed the rest. *I* needed the rest, but I had to drive.

I stretched out hands stiff from clutching the steering wheel of my trusty, rusty Honda, the caboose in our little convoy. My husband, Dan, headed the procession, pulling the stock trailer holding stage one of our earthly goods. Next came his brother-in-law Gerrit, pulling his own stock trailer loaded with our earthly goods stage two.

I had each bar, each bolt, each spot of rust on Gerrit's trailer indelibly imprinted on my brain. Counting the bolt heads distracted me from the dread that clawed at me whenever I saw the empty road stretching endlessly ahead of me.

A road that wound crazily through pine-covered mountains, then wide open, almost barren, plains. Now, on the last leg of our journey, we were driving through ploughed and open fields broken only by arrow-straight fence lines and meandering cottonwoods. Tender green leaves misted the bare branches of the poplars edging the road, creating a promise of spring that I hadn't counted on spending here.

I hadn't gone silently down this road. I had balked, kicked, and pleaded. I had even dared to pray that a God I didn't talk to often would intervene.

Of course I was bucking some pretty powerful intercessors. I'm sure the entire VandeKeere family was united in their prayers for their beloved brother, son, cousin, nephew, and grandchild to be enfolded once again in the bosom of the family and the farm where they thought he belonged. So it was a safe bet my flimsy request lay buried in the avalanche of petitions flowing from Holmes Crossing.

The one person I had on my side was my sister, Terra. But she only talked to God when she'd had too much to drink. Of course, in that state, she chatted up anyone who would listen.

The friends I left behind in Vancouver were sympathetic, but they all thought this trip would be an adventure. *Interesting* adventure, my friend Josie had said when I told her.

I glanced in the rearview mirror at my sleeping children. Nicholas shifted in his car seat, his sticky hands clutching a soggy Popsicle stick. The Popsicle had been a blatant bribe, and the oblong purple stain running over his coat from chin to belly would probably not wash out. A constant reminder of my giving in.

Since Edmonton, I'd been tweaking my introduction, and now that we had turned off the highway, time and miles ate up what time I had left. I had only ten minutes to convince myself that I'd sooner be heading toward the intersection of "no" and "where," otherwise known as Holmes Crossing, Alberta, than back to Vancouver.

We would still be there if it weren't for Lonnie Dansworth--snake, scumbag, and crooked building contractor. The $90,000's worth of unpaid bills he left in the "VandeKeere Motors" inbox tipped Dan's fledgling mechanic business from barely getting by to going under. The Dansworth Debacle, in turn, wiped out the finely drawn pictures I'd created in my head of the dream life and home Dan and I had been saving for. The home that represented stability for a marriage that had wobbled on shaky ground the past year.

The second push to Holmes Crossing came when Dan's stepfather, Keith Cook, booked a midlife crisis that resulted in him doing a boot-scootin' boogie out of hearth, home, Holmes Crossing, and the family farm, leaving a vacuum in the VandeKeere family's life that Dan decided we would temporarily fill.

Temporary had been a recurring refrain in our life so far. The first two years of our marriage, Dan had worked for a small garage in Markham while I worked in the ER at the Scarborough Hospital. When an oil company needed a maintenance mechanic, we moved to Fort McMurray, and I got a job as a camp nurse. Two years later, an opportunity to be his own boss came up in Vancouver. When we packed up and moved, Dan promised me this was our final destination. Until now.

"It's only a year," Dan assured me when he laid off the employees, pulled out of the lease on the shop, and filed away the blueprints we had been drawing up for our dream home. We could have lived off my salary while Dan got his feet under him and worked on our relationship away from the outside influences of a mother Dan still called twice a week. But Dan's restless heart wasn't in it. Being a mechanic had never been his dream. Though I'd heard plenty of negative stories about his stepfather, Keith, a wistful yearning for the farm of his youth wove through his complaints. We were torn just like the adage said: "Men mourn for what they lost, women for what they haven't got."

The final push came when a seemingly insignificant matter caught my attention. The garage's bilingual secretary, Keely. She could talk "mechanic" and "Dan," and the few times I stopped at the garage, she would chat me up in a falsely bright voice while her eyes followed Dan's movements around the shop.

When her name showed up too often on our call display, I confronted Dan. He admitted he'd been spending time with her. Told me he was lonely. He also told me that he had made a mistake. That he was trying to break things off with her. He was adamant that they'd never been physically intimate. Never even kissed her, he claimed. She was just someone he spent time with.

I tried not to take on the fault for our slow drift away from each other or the casual treatment of our relationship as kids and work and trying to put money aside for our future slowly sunk its demanding claws into our lives, slowly pulling us in separate directions.

I also reminded him that I had remained faithful, taking the righteous high road. Dan was chastened, Keely quit, and her name never came up again. But her shadowy presence still hovered between us, making Dan contrite, and me wary.

Now, with each stop that brought us closer to the farm and Holmes Crossing and the possibility of repairing our broken relationship, I'd seen Dan's smile grow deeper, softer. The lines edging his mouth smoothed away, the nervous tic in the corner of one eye disappeared.

Mine grew worse.

A soft sigh pulled my eyes toward the back seat. Anneke still lay slack jawed, her blanket curled around her fist. Nicholas stirred again, a deep V digging into his brow, his bottom lip pushed out in a glistening pout. Nicholas was a pretty child, but his transition from sleep to waking was an ugly battle he fought with intense tenacity.

I had only minutes before the troops were fully engaged.

My previous reluctance to arrive at the farm now morphed into desperation for survival. I stomped on the gas pedal, swung around the two horse trailers, and bulleted down the hill into the valley toward my home for the next year.

My cell phone trilled. I grabbed it off the dashboard, glancing sidelong at Nicholas as I did.

"What's up?" Dan's tinny voice demanded. "What's your rush?"

"The boy is waking up," I whispered, gauging how long I had before his angry wails filled the car.

"Just let him cry."

I didn't mean to sigh. Truly I didn't. But it zipped past my pressed-together lips. In that too-deep-for-words escape of my breath, Dan heard an entire conversation.

"Honestly, Leslie, you've got to learn to ignore--"

Dear Lord, forgive me. I hung up. And then I turned my phone off.

DEAR READER

You met Claire in the book Close to His Heart. And you also met Cory in Divided Hearts.

Those two stories came together in this book. When I wrote Cory's story, I spoke of the hero she had always hoped would come into her life. That hero always took the form of her brother. Now, I finally got to finish that story and tell you more about Claire.

I hope you enjoyed reading Claire and Nik's story. I often buy books based on other people's reviews so I'm hoping you're willing to leave one on this book to give future readers some idea of what to expect.

OTHER SERIES

Introducing a new series called

FAMILY TIES

Four siblings trying to finding their way back to family and faith

#1 A COWBOY'S REUNION

He's still reeling from the breakup. She's ashamed of what she did. Can a chance reunion mend the fence, or are some hearts forever broken? If you like second chance stories, buried passions, and big country settings, then you'll love this emotional novel.

#2 THE COWBOY'S FAMILY

She's desperate. He's loyal. Will a dark lie hold them back from finding love on the ranch? If you like determined heroines, charming cowboys, and family dramas, then you'll love this heartfelt novel.

#3 TAMING THE COWBOY

A saddle bronc trying to prove himself worthy to a father who never loved him. A wedding planner whose ex-fiancee was too busy chasing his own dreams to think of hers. Two people, completely wrong for each other who yet need each other in ways they never realized. Can they let go of their own plans to find a way to heal together?

#4 THE COWBOY'S RETURN

He enlisted in the military, leaving his one true love behind.

She gave herself to a lesser man and paid a terrible price.

In their hometown of Rockyview, they can choose to come together or say a final goodbye...

* * *

SWEETHEARTS OF SWEET CREEK

#1 HOMECOMING

Will past bitterness blind her to future love?

#2 - HER HEARTS PROMISE

When the man she once loved reveals a hidden truth about the past, Nadine has to choose between justice and love.

#3 - CLOSE TO HIS HEART

Can love triumph over tragedy?

#4 - DIVIDED HEARTS

To embrace a second chance at love, they'll need to discover the truths of the past and the possibilities of the future...

#5 - A HERO AT HEART

If you like rekindled chemistry, family drama, and small, beautiful towns, then you'll love this story of heart and heroism.

#6 - A MOTHER'S HEART

If you like matchmaking daughters, heartfelt stories of mending broken homes, and fixer-upper romance, then this story of second chances is just right for you.

* * *

HOLMES CROSSING SERIES

#1 THE ONLY BEST PLACE

One mistake jeopardized their relationship. Will surrendering her dreams to save their marriage destroy her?

#2 ALL IN ONE PLACE

She has sass, spunk and a haunting secret.

#3 THIS PLACE

Her secret could destroy their second chance at love

#4 A SILENCE IN THE HEART

Can a little boy, an injured kitten and a concerned vet

with his own past pain, break down the walls of Tracy's heart?

#5 ANY MAN OF MINE

Living with three brothers has made Danielle tired of guys and cowboys. She wants a man. But is she making the right choice?

ABOUT THE AUTHOR

Carolyne Aarsen was a city girl until a tall, blonde and handsome man entered her life and she convinced him to marry her and he did. Then he brought her to live on a farm where her resume garnered some interesting entries. Growing a garden, sewing blue jeans, baking, pickling and preserving. She learned how to handle cows, ride a horse, drive tractors, snow machines and a John Deere loader. Together they raised four amazing children and took in foster children. Somewhere in all this she learned to write. Her stories show a love of open spaces, the fellowship of her Christian community and the gift God has given us in Christ.

To find out more about Carolyne and get a free e-book go to:

www.carolyneaarsen.com
carolynewriter@xplornet.ca

EXCERPT - THE ONLY BEST PLACE

The Only Best Place is the first book in the Holmes Crossing Series.

Smile. Think happy thoughts. Take a deep breath and...

"Hello. I'm Leslie VandeKeere, and I'm a farmer's wife."

No. No. All wrong. That sounds like I'm addressing a self-help group for stressed-out urban dwellers.

I angled the rearview mirror of my car to do a sincerity check on my expression and pulled a face at my reflection. Brown eyes. Brown hair. Both the polar opposite of the VandeKeere signature blonde hair and blue eyes repeated throughout the Dutch-based community of Holmes Crossing.

During the past hour of the long drive from Vancouver to here, I'd been practicing my introduction to varied and sundry members of the vast community of which I knew about four and a half people. I'd been trying out various intros. That last one was a bust. I'd never been a farmer's wife. Would never be a farmer's wife. I'm a nurse, even though my focus the next year was supposed to be on our marriage. Not my career.

I cleared my throat and tried again. "Our year here will be interesting."

Worse yet. Most women could break that code faster than you could say "fifteen percent off." *Interesting* was a twilight word that either veered toward the good or the dark side.

Right now my delivery was a quiet and subdued Darth Vader.

I had to keep my voice down so I wouldn't wake my two kids. After four *Veggie Tales* and a couple of off-key renditions of "The Itsy Bitsy Spider," they had finally drifted off to sleep, and I didn't want to risk waking them. The eighteen hour trip had been hard on us. They needed the rest. *I* needed the rest, but I had to drive.

I stretched out hands stiff from clutching the

steering wheel of my trusty, rusty Honda, the caboose in our little convoy. My husband, Dan, headed the procession, pulling the stock trailer holding stage one of our earthly goods. Next came his brother-in-law Gerrit, pulling his own stock trailer loaded with our earthly goods stage two.

I had each bar, each bolt, each spot of rust on Gerrit's trailer indelibly imprinted on my brain. Counting the bolt heads distracted me from the dread that clawed at me whenever I saw the empty road stretching endlessly ahead of me.

A road that wound crazily through pine-covered mountains, then wide open, almost barren, plains. Now, on the last leg of our journey, we were driving through ploughed and open fields broken only by arrow-straight fence lines and meandering cottonwoods. Tender green leaves misted the bare branches of the poplars edging the road, creating a promise of spring that I hadn't counted on spending here.

I hadn't gone silently down this road. I had balked, kicked, and pleaded. I had even dared to pray that a God I didn't talk to often would intervene.

Of course I was bucking some pretty powerful intercessors. I'm sure the entire VandeKeere family was united in their prayers for their beloved brother, son, cousin, nephew, and grandchild to be enfolded once again in the bosom of the family and the farm where they thought he belonged. So it was a safe bet my flimsy request lay buried in the avalanche of petitions flowing from Holmes Crossing.

The one person I had on my side was my sister, Terra. But she only talked to God when she'd had too much to drink. Of course, in that state, she chatted up anyone who would listen.

The friends I left behind in Vancouver were sympathetic, but they all thought this trip would be an adventure. *Interesting* adventure, my friend Josie had said when I told her.

I glanced in the rearview mirror at my sleeping children. Nicholas shifted in his car seat, his sticky hands clutching a soggy Popsicle stick. The Popsicle had been a blatant bribe, and the oblong purple stain running over his coat from chin to belly would probably not wash out. A constant reminder of my giving in.

Since Edmonton, I'd been tweaking my introduction, and now that we had turned off the highway, time and miles ate up what time I had left. I had only ten minutes to convince myself that I'd sooner be heading toward the intersection of "no" and "where," otherwise known as Holmes Crossing, Alberta, than back to Vancouver.

We would still be there if it weren't for Lonnie Dansworth--snake, scumbag, and crooked building contractor. The $90,000's worth of unpaid bills he left in the "VandeKeere Motors" inbox tipped Dan's fledgling mechanic business from barely getting by to going under. The Dansworth Debacle, in turn, wiped out the finely drawn pictures I'd created in my head of the dream life and home Dan and I had been saving for. The home that represented stability for a marriage that had wobbled on shaky ground the past year.

The second push to Holmes Crossing came when Dan's stepfather, Keith Cook, booked a midlife crisis that resulted in him doing a boot-scootin' boogie out of hearth, home, Holmes Crossing, and the family farm, leaving a vacuum in the VandeKeere family's life that Dan decided we would temporarily fill.

Temporary had been a recurring refrain in our life so far. The first two years of our marriage, Dan had worked for a small garage in Markham while I worked in the ER at the Scarborough Hospital. When an oil company needed a maintenance mechanic, we moved to Fort McMurray, and I got a job as a camp nurse. Two years later, an opportunity to be his own boss came up in Vancouver. When we packed up and moved, Dan promised me this was our final destination. Until now.

"It's only a year," Dan assured me when he laid off the employees, pulled out of the lease on the shop, and filed away the blueprints we had been drawing up for our dream home. We could have lived off my salary while Dan got his feet under him and worked on our relationship away from the outside influences of a mother Dan still called twice a week. But Dan's restless heart wasn't in it. Being a mechanic had never been his dream. Though I'd heard plenty of negative stories about his stepfather, Keith, a wistful yearning for the farm of his youth wove through his complaints. We were torn just like the adage said: "Men mourn for what they lost, women for what they haven't got."

The final push came when a seemingly insignificant matter caught my attention. The garage's bilingual secretary, Keely. She could talk "mechanic" and "Dan," and the few times I stopped at the garage, she would chat me up in a falsely bright voice while her eyes followed Dan's movements around the shop.

When her name showed up too often on our call display, I confronted Dan. He admitted he'd been spending time with her. Told me he was lonely. He also told me that he had made a mistake. That he was trying to break things off with her. He was adamant that they'd never been physically intimate. Never even kissed her, he claimed. She was just someone he spent time with.

I tried not to take on the fault for our slow drift away from each other or the casual treatment of our relationship as kids and work and trying to put money aside for our future slowly sunk its demanding claws into our lives, slowly pulling us in separate directions.

I also reminded him that I had remained faithful, taking the righteous high road. Dan was chastened, Keely quit, and her name never came up again. But her shadowy presence still hovered between us, making Dan contrite, and me wary.

Now, with each stop that brought us closer to the farm and Holmes Crossing and the possibility of repairing our broken relationship, I'd seen Dan's smile grow deeper, softer. The lines edging his mouth smoothed away, the nervous tic in the corner of one eye disappeared.

Mine grew worse.

A soft sigh pulled my eyes toward the back seat. Anneke still lay slack jawed, her blanket curled around her fist. Nicholas stirred again, a deep V digging into his brow, his bottom lip pushed out in a glistening pout. Nicholas was a pretty child, but his transition from sleep to waking was an ugly battle he fought with intense tenacity.

I had only minutes before the troops were fully engaged.

My previous reluctance to arrive at the farm now morphed into desperation for survival. I stomped on the gas pedal, swung around the two horse trailers, and bulleted down the hill into the valley toward my home for the next year.

My cell phone trilled. I grabbed it off the dashboard, glancing sidelong at Nicholas as I did.

"What's up?" Dan's tinny voice demanded. "What's your rush?"

"The boy is waking up," I whispered, gauging how long I had before his angry wails filled the car.

"Just let him cry."

I didn't mean to sigh. Truly I didn't. But it

zipped past my pressed-together lips. In that too-deep-for-words escape of my breath, Dan heard an entire conversation.

"Honestly, Leslie, you've got to learn to ignore--"

Dear Lord, forgive me. I hung up. And then I turned my phone off.

To purchase, go to Amazon.com and search The Only Best Place.

DISCLAIMER

All characters in this book have no existence outside the imagination of the author and have no relation whatsoever to anyone bearing the same name or names. They are not even distantly inspired by any individual known or unknown to the author, and all incidents are pure invention.

Made in the USA
Las Vegas, NV
11 August 2022

53107859R00215